the silent, subtle,
ever-present perils
of life

the silent, subtle, ever-present perils of life

A NOVEL

Alcy Leyva

GREEN WRITERS PRESS *Brattleboro, Vermont*

Printed in the United States

10 9 8 7 6 5 4 3 2 1

Green Writers Press is a Vermont-based publisher whose mission is to
spread a message of hope and renewal through the words and images we
publish. Throughout, we will adhere to our commitment to preserving and
protecting the natural resources of the earth. To that end, a percentage
of our proceeds will be donated to environmental activist groups and
social justice organizations. Green Writers Press gratefully acknowledges
support from individual donors, friends, and readers to help support the
environment and our publishing initiative.

Giving Voice to Writers & Artists Who Will Make the World a Better Place
Green Writers Press | Brattleboro, Vermont
www.greenwriterspress.com

ISBN: 979-8-9870707-4-1

COVER ART: Kehinde Wiley
The Herring Net (Zakary Antoine and Samedy Pierre Louisson), 2017.
© Kehinde Wiley. Courtesy of Stephen Friedman Gallery, London.

PRINTED ON PAPER WITH PULP THAT COMES FROM FSC-CERTIFIED FORESTS, MANAGED FORESTS
THAT GUARANTEE RESPONSIBLE ENVIRONMENTAL, SOCIAL, AND ECONOMIC PRACTICES.

For Avery, Aiden, Rene, and MA.
If you brave that ocean,
I promise to come and find you.

And for my dad.
Who built his raft and took to the waters
for his own miracle.

Consider the subtleness of the sea; how its most dreaded creatures glide under water, unapparent for the most part, and treacherously hidden beneath the loveliest tints of azure. Consider also the devilish brilliance and beauty of many of its most remorseless tribes, as the dainty embellished shape of many species of sharks. Consider, once more, the universal cannibalism of the sea; all whose creatures prey upon each other, carrying on eternal war since the world began.

Consider all this; and then turn to the green, gentle, and most docile earth; consider them both, the sea and the land; and do you not find a strange analogy to something in yourself? For as this appalling ocean surrounds the verdant land, so in the soul of man there lies one insular Tahiti, full of peace and joy, but encompassed by all the horrors of the half-known life. God keep thee! Push not off from that isle, thou canst never return!

—HERMAN MELVILLE

the silent, subtle,
ever-present perils
of life

~ ~ ~

Prologue ⤳

MAJI wakes with the sting of seawater in his nose and stiff pain in his neck—a product of falling asleep on the wooden floor of his makeshift raft. He wipes away at the splinters digging into his cheek as a growl reaches up from the hollow pit of his stomach.

Over the edge of his raft, in the hazy distance, the New York City skyline is nothing more than a black bar on the horizon. Maji realizes that in the panic to get out onto the water, he's left his glasses at home, right where he has always left them: the rickety, old bookshelf between his room and his mother's room.

Seeing that his raft is now overlooking the coast of Coney Island, Maji marvels at how far he's come. Just a few days before, he admired how the amusement park rides swerved and dipped through the air. Now, miles away from the shore, his terrible eyesight hides the monstrous shadows of the park's roller coaster and Ferris wheel. Maji has never been on a Coney Island ride. And with this comes an avalanche of other "never wills."

He will never see his mom again.
Never taste her cooking.
Never hit a game-winning jump shot to end a pickup game in The Cage.

Maji loves that court. It's his favorite place to be on those long summer days when the heat seems to reach out of the cement and strangle your ankles. But Maji can't ball at all. He can barely bounce one without the ball jumping up and smacking him. Of course, that doesn't stop him from dreaming of running up and down that court and hearing the crowd cheer—just a Bronx boy dreaming now.

Maji looks at the lapping waters around his boat and is happy that his little vessel isn't taking in water. It had taken him only a few days to gather the materials (helped by a search or two on YouTube), but Maji was proud of his tiny ship. Not bad for a kid from the Melville Projects.

After taking inventory in his food pack (i.e., a Nike duffle bag filled with junk food), Maji opens a bag of cheese doodles and unfolds the map he had printed for his trip out on the floor of the raft. Pinning one of its edges down with his sneakers, Maji places his phone next to the paper and swipes the screen to his virtual map.

His original plan was to sail out of Soundview, follow it down from the Bronx River to the East River, and follow it south, passing Rikers and under all the bridges (Manhattan, Brooklyn) until he got out to sea.

That *was* the original plan.

What saved him some time instead was lugging his gear out to the Hudson, not an easy task but worth it in the long run. He had brought the raft out in pieces over two days; barrels, rope, wooden planks, and broomsticks. He hid them all under a poncho by the water between trips. The raft had taken him three hours to build.

He pushed his clunky boat out into the water at around midnight. The New York City summer felt like it was about to burn down the whole city. Along with the 100-degree weather, Maji had heard of four planned protests in the five boroughs. The previous night's gathering, which featured hundreds of people walking across the Brooklyn Bridge, quickly turned into a total riot. The images of police on horseback, clouds of tear gas, and bloodied people running for their lives had made Maji sick to his stomach. The only silver lining was that no one would notice a sixteen-year-old black boy sailing down the middle of the Hudson.

Maji found dragging his makeshift boat down to the launch point challenging. By the time he reached the water's edge, blisters were forming on his fingers. Pushing the raft out onto the water set a dull pain in his stomach and back. The makeshift raft bobbed up and down for a while, with Maji just staring at it, holding his breath, hoping the whole thing wouldn't just sink. But the knots, the wood, the planks, and the barrels—they held, and he was able to take a breath.

And then Maji was off, gripped in the current of the Hudson as it dragged him between the lights of New York to his left and Jersey to his right. To him, the skyscrapers and buildings looked like mirrors stacked into giant towers. Each lit square hummed and flickered in the night air as if invisible music bounced between their panes.

Following his printed map, the new route was a straight shot south, passing Governor's Island and out into the Lower Bay. Maji had built oars out of brooms and plastic sheets for paddling and steering, but it was like his raft knew the route. He only had to manage one bridge before reaching the bays into the Atlantic. Then, with the ocean spread out before him and his muscles burning, Maji laid his head down to rest.

According to his cell phone, that was three hours ago.

Like a proper captain, Maji takes a quick inventory of his things. His bag of snacks—check. His book, his map, his phone—check, check, check. The phone battery was at 97%. He left the screen unlocked—*it's not like someone will steal it out here, anyway.* And it wasn't like he was going to be making calls. He considered that service would probably be a problem out on the water. But his cellphone does provide him a light source, a GPS to compare to his printed map, and of course, his music collection—something he treasures above anything. That's all he needs.

Maji wonders how far out to sea he will need to see it. *How long does it take for a miracle?* he thinks.

But then his mind bends, skipping back across his memory to the sound of splashing water. Out in the darkness, he sees the image of a pregnant woman holding her hands to her chest. There's nothing around her, but Maji can feel his terror as if it's strangling him. There's another ghostly image just a few feet in front of her. A gun. A white hand. She opens her mouth to yell.

Before the gun fires, Maji feels the air change and turns to face the horizon.

The water grows quiet. The sky appears to bruise.

This is it, Maji tells himself. *It's here already—the miracle.*

A red eye creeps out of the water in the distance and swells—its vast light changes the entire sky. No, it's not an eye, but Maji knows it is beautiful. He doesn't blink. Instead, he stands to his feet and watches, mouth open.

The clouds bend towards the sun as the new day is born.

Maji looks over to where the screaming woman had appeared, but she's escaped with the darkness.

Pulling his earbuds from his pocket, Maji plugs himself into his phone and slips them in. He plays the first

song on the playlist. As if fate, the first song that plays is
Frank Ocean.

Maybe it's fate, but he sings along. And then it gets to
the part where Frank sings:

And the water is exactly what I wanted
It's everything I thought it would be
But this neighborhood is gettin' trippier every day
The neighborhood is going ape-shit crazy

Maji laughs out loud and catches himself when he realizes that he's been crying this entire time. He has never
known the world to be so warm and beautiful. And in this
new life revealing itself to him, he finds himself ready to
find his miracle.

Part 1 ~~~

The Boy

Chapter 1 ⤳

Fifteen days before Maji pushes down the Hudson...

MAJI's earbuds are in and his head is down as he walks to class. The weird nightmare he had last night is still making its way through his nerves, but the music pushes back these thoughts. He weaves in and out of the other kids, opting to skip the early morning chat and gossip rounds.

As he walks, Maji stares at his phone as he swipes through his usual social media rounds.

IG is dead.

No new music out.

He checks his DM's as if expecting to hear from someone.

Luckily, Consciousness 2.0 had posted something overnight. Maji waits for the video to load with almost nervous energy. Not only is this guy the most popular vlogger on YouTube, but he's also only two years older than Maji and seems to be living the life. He had started with a channel based on his video game kill montages set to corny trap music—the kind of videos everyone was putting out at the time. But after one of his impersonation videos went viral, everything fell into place.

Seventy million subscribers later, C2.0 (as everyone started calling him) is one of the biggest names on the internet. He posts three weekly videos and switches them up every time: anime, video games, movies, politics, and new kicks. He always speaks the truth about how he feels. Maji watches his channel religiously; in his mind, Consciousness 2.0 is the epitome of success.

C2.0 leaps onto his usual gaming chair and spins around, barking like a dog. He's wearing a black and white "OBEY" shirt and a fresh Yankee fit (C.20 lives out of Brooklyn). Maji curls his lips to keep from laughing out loud. The guy's room features an anime poster of Guts hanging over a large bed with a red comforter.

C.20 starts by thanking all his followers and giving shout-outs to his sponsors before getting to his main talking point.

"Alright, y'all. Here is my question. What is the best

superhero movie and why is it still not better than *Black Panther?*" He laughs, and Maji laughs with him as he turns the corner toward his first class. C.20 taps his temple and winks at the camera. "Let me tell you right now—I bet the higher-ups, the powers that be, don't want to make a sequel. That joint woke up too many people. You see everything going on outside? Do you see what happened to that kid in Florida? No way do they want us out here feelin' like we can be superheroes. No way." With his usual crazy energy, C2.0 starts flexing and punching the air.

Maji laughs and pauses the video to track down the clip C2.0 is referencing. After several selfies and status updates, he stops at a video posted by a friend of a friend under the title "FLORIDA SKATE."

Hoping to see something dumb to pass the time, Maji watches a blurry video of a police chase. It's bodycam footage of a cop running after what looks like a black kid just a little older than Maji riding a skateboard. The camera is shaking, and the clattering of the cop's belt drowns out what he's yelling.

The cop stops running and points a gun at the boy's back.

Maji closes the screen and slides his phone into his pocket. It isn't like he doesn't know that this is happening—the violence on the streets, cops shooting black people left and right. It's just that he doesn't like seeing it on his feed all the time. Social media is always overflowing with either stupid cat videos or people dying. Sometimes, Maji stays away from online chat to protect his mental health.

Mr. DaCosta, Maji's English teacher, is leaning against the doorway when Maji arrives. He's wearing a simple blue button-down shirt and a black tie with slacks. Out of all the teachers in the school, Maji feels that Mr. D's dress is always the sharpest. He sports slicked-back brown hair and a black beard whose edges are turning white. His glasses dangle on the edge of his nose. He's holding his silver coffee mug in one hand while his other is free for an early morning fist bump.

He meets his eyes with Maji, and his lips slide to the side of his face as if he has something to say.

Maji thinks he knows what this is about.

"I forgot the book today, Mr. D. But I promise that I'm almost done with it. I just got a few chapters left."

A month ago, Maji had posed a challenge that he knew Mr. DaCosta couldn't turn down. If Maji read three "classics" outside of class, Mr. D. would have to play him in ball in front of the whole school. Sure, he had no idea how good his teacher was on the court, but it was the type of challenge he knew no one from the Bronx could turn down. It was a matter of pride. Maji hadn't read a book in its entirety since middle school, but he dedicated himself to get through the books page-by-page, line-by-line. He finished *The Great Gatsby* in two weeks. *Don Quixote* in a week and a half. And though this latest book is turning out to be more enjoyable than the others, it's proven harder than those first two combined.

Mr. D. takes a sip of his coffee. "Good to know, but that's not what I was about to ask. Mind telling me why you were on in-school suspension yesterday?"

Maji feels his face get hot. "I told Ms. Finn to shut up." As soon as Mr. D gives him the look he usually gives him, he quickly adds, "It wasn't even a big deal. You don't understand. She called me 'boy'. I ain't nobody's 'boy'."

Mr. D. sighs. "That temper, man. And I'm not saying you were wrong. I'll do my part and see what happened. But remember what I taught you. Regardless if you feel you're being disrespected, there's a right way and a wrong way to do things. And you can sigh and shrug your shoulders all you want, but you know we've been working on this since day one. What happens when you're out there and someone gets in your face?"

Maji can only see Ms. Finn smile as he packed his books and left the room. She hates him. He doesn't know how to tell Mr. D. this, but Maji knows. Ever since he started school, Ms. Finn always looked at Maji's hands to check if he was stealing. She was always commenting on his hair. Each one felt like a sharp nail chipping into his skin.

Maji grits his teeth together as his says, "Trust me. No one's going to want to get in my face, Mister."

But Mr. D looks unamused. He was born and raised in the Bronx, just a few blocks from the Melville Projects. In a building where more than half of the teachers are white, having a Puerto Rican teacher from the block who knows a good chop cheese hits differently.

"Because what—you'll punch them? Look around, Maji. What happens when you're in a position where your fist and your word mean nothing? That's what I want you to be ready for. Inside these walls, Maji, you can make mistakes. But I want you to be ready for the real world. The future, man. I'm not always going to be around to keep reminding you to use your head. Lock that down."

Maji wants to roll his eyes but knows better in front of Mr. DaCosta. While he understands that his teacher means well, Maji feels like there are thousands of Finns out there in the world. The news is filled with Finns. Social Media. Music. Everyday is something new. School shootings, politics, scandals. But Maji feels like all of these things are not part of the world he lives in. He's just a junior in high school. Ms. Finn's classroom was always a class he could walk out of. To him, college is a lifetime away. Future? That only gives him more anxiety. His parents, his teachers, his counselors—everyone keeps telling him that things are going to change when he leaves high school. To Maji, this seems too outside of him to care.

"I *am* locking it down. Nobody's going to be disrespecting or talking down to me, Mister. And what do you mean you're not going to be around? We still got senior year to go, Mr. D. One whole year. You're not going to get rid of me that easy."

Instead of his usual sarcasm, Maji senses a change in

the man's body. Mr. DaCosta grows so silent that Maji feels as if the man has vanished right in front of his eyes. Before he can ask, the school bell rings for homeroom, and a steady stream of students files into the room. Mr. D gives them fist bumps as the color returns to his face.

As Maji prepares for class, he can't help but feel like he's said something wrong.

Chapter 2 ⌒

Thirteen days before Maji crafted a ship to find the end of the ocean . . .

For the second night in a row, Maji dreams an impossible dream.

He feels a weight set into his skin, pushing his entire body into his bed's mattress. And as the folds of fabric slowly swallow him, he suddenly feels as if he's underwater.
No. Thicker than water.
Tar. Blood.

Maji opens his eyes, seeing a dark, endless ocean sur-rounding him. His first instinct is to swim, to wave and thrash about, but the substance holds him still. The warmth coils over his neck and ankles. It makes him listen.

A deep, guttural sound echoes in the darkness.

Colorful spouts of air reach out like tendrils to grasp him. To pull him closer.

The ocean speaks his name.

Maji falls out of his bed, gasping for air. His clothes are drenched with sweat, and foam has formed in his mouth, making it hard to breathe. Wheezing, he looks at the window of his room as the rain leaves, snaking trails down its side. Pathways of water leading down to the same point.

Maji feels his body heavy as he goes to school the follow-ing day. Another nightmare-filled night, another long slog of classes ahead. What makes things even more unbear-able is that all of New York is talking about the Florida video. It leaps at him from newspaper covers as he passes newsstands. It flashes on cell phone screens as people wait for their turns on crosswalks. Maji can't count the number of times cops have shot someone who looked like him. He knows that bad things happen to peo-ple. His mom had a chain ripped off her neck in broad daylight just one block from his home. Police spotlights occasionally light up his block as if treating black people like roaches is the best solution to crime. Everyone in the neighborhood knows the difference between the sound of firecrackers and a gun.

In the Bronx, it rains. It snows. Sometimes there's no water. No heat. That's just the way of life. Shootings are no different. The folks holding the guns sometimes wear blue uniforms and gold shields.

Maji remembers that his mom commented about every story that crept up between the sidewalk slabs. She would shake her head and suck her teeth whenever someone got gunned down. But the cop shootings made her even more unsettled. She would keep comments about these events to herself, but Maji had eyes that could see past the layers of his mom's skin.

After some time, even she grew numb to it all.

Coincidence is becoming life. The cops serve and protect, Maji knows, but they can shoot you someday.

That's why this recent shooting isn't surprising to him. It isn't shocking to believe that anyone could be in the crosshairs. What was surprising was the reaction.

Social media exploded with calls to fire the police officers and put them on trial. The video spread like wildfire. Again, nothing unusual. But the voices grew and grew. Only two days after the video goes viral, Maji hears of the first protest in Orlando. The fact that everyone is all hot about something that happens all the time confuses him. *What about the other folks that have been shot over the last year?*

Of course, the only reason Maji knows their names is because of Mr. D's class. *You have to know what's going on;* he hears him say. *And when you feel that you can, you have to do something about it.*

Maji tries not to read too much into the protests. And he's not alone. None of his high school friends bring it up. Florida might as well be another planet. But while Mr. D seemed to be the only one giving a damn, Maji continued with his life. His mom doesn't bring it up, and his dad . . .

Maji doesn't even want to know what his father has to say.

Everyone would forget in a few days. Not out of malice or anything. It's just the way things work.

"It's like people want to forget," he says when it comes up in his English class that afternoon.

Mr. D rubs his beard with his glasses. "And why do you think people want to forget?"

Maji thinks for a long time before responding. "Because it's like they have to forget. Because if you're in pain and if you can't do nothing with the pain, you have to try to forget it."

The protest signs will come down.
The hashtags will disappear.
The names will be forgotten.
This, too, will pass.

Chapter 3 ⤳

Twelve days before Maji went out to sea. . .

MAJI stands on the train platform staring at his screen as C2.0 wraps up Maji's favorite segment, "Bodega Chef." In it, the YouTuber tries to make a three-course meal using only ingredients from the local bodega (nine times out of ten, he throws up). C2.0 then closes this installment with his usual shout-outs.

"Real talk. A big, massive shout-out to everyone who came up and showed your boy love last night in Queens. I can't thank y'all enough for the support you've shown me and my channel. C2.0 Nation is the best. Let's spread the word about police violence wherever we can, right?" He then flashes his trademark C2 sign and a smile.

As the silver five train pulls into Maji's station, he wonders how it feels to have so many friends. C2.0 has it all. As a full-time streamer, he dropped out of school after one semester to focus on building his channel. At eighteen, C.20 is a YouTube icon. In his mind, Maji dreams of the day he can meet C2.0 in person, and they would hit it off because Maji knows everything about him. It was just a matter of time.

Maji slips his phone back into his pocket and takes more interest in his surroundings. There must be a Yankee game today because there's barely room to stand on the platform. Instead, Maji feels surrounded by a sea of faces and conversations he either can't understand or doesn't care about: dating apps, office parties, politics, and alehouses.

Maji has never gone to a Yankee game. But, contrary to popular belief, being from the Bronx doesn't mean that's something you can do. Back in the day, if you were lucky, someone on the block got a hookup from their job or someone inside the stadium. That was the old Yankee Stadium—when there was a fair mix of people coming from Uptown, Downtown, and out-of-town. But as soon as the new stadium went up, Maji noticed fewer and fewer folks with his skin color dressed in pinstripes.

Of course, Maji knows that if he ever wants to see a baseball game, his father's job could make that happen.

But the last thing Maji wants to do is ask that man for anything.

As he boards the train, the rowdy crowd pushes in behind him. The mass of people, with their newly bought Yankee-fitted water bottles, have loud conversations that fill the car with a sea of sound. Then, finally, someone breaks into a "Let's Go Yankees!" chant, and the train gets swept up.

Maji watches them from a distance, watches the swell of the crowd grow, and he braces himself as their feelings pour into him like an avalanche of sound and color.

Purple.

Crunchy.

Static.

Maji has never told anyone that he sometimes can sense these things. Part of it is that Maji finds it hard to describe the sounds and colors that float by his eyes. The easiest way would be that, on occasion, he could see and feel people's emotions. Sometimes they look like clouds that make his tongue feel prickly. Sometimes they appear as flashing sirens that sprout up in his mind when people shout or cry.

Maji first noticed how his senses could read the world around age five. His mother was hanging up Christmas decorations and accidentally glanced the living room radiator which, in any Projects, is either bone cold or scalding hot. The metal burned a half-moon into her calf that Maji would later trace with his finger when they watched movies together on the couch. But what Maji remembered more was her scream—one that sent a wave into him like a brushfire. It took him years to learn to shut the loud sounds and colors out of his mind—mainly because he didn't want his parents sending him to some doctor who would throw medications at him. So instead, he worked on his thoughts and anxiety and put up thick walls to protect himself. The fact that Maji can sense the feelings of everyone in that train car tells him that he's tired and needs sleep.

At the Yankee Stadium stop, the loud group spills onto the platform and makes lines to climb the staircase. The car is finally quiet, and Maji's vision returns to Earth. A short while later, the subway turns into the El. Now perched high on the rattling, green iron-work tracks over-looking the Bronx, the train's thick windows fill with rays of sunshine. To Maji, the stubby, brown buildings of his borough line the train's path like a runway.

Maji takes in each stop as if remembering the places he's been. Even though his school is in Harlem, Maji's heart and home are in the crooked sidewalks and spouting fire hydrants of the Bronx. Every avenue has its own story to him.

Jackson Ave is where Maji's oldest friend, Crespo, lives.

Prospect Avenue always has the most live summer block parties.

Because it's mostly long stretches of unused factory buildings and empty lots, Intervale Ave was home to most of the gangs in the Bronx back in the day. Now it's mainly used for drag racing on the weekends. Mr. D grew up here.

Simpson Avenue is the shopping area—you need something, you stop there.

This is the recipe of the Bronx: beauty and struggle, all huddled under the same umbrella. Every block has its very own projects, personality, and people. The winding path of the train continues until you reach the heart of the South Bronx—Park South.

Maji gets off and passes someone at the turnstile asking for a free swipe to get on the train. The NYPD hates giving people free rides, so every time Maji does, he feels like he's flipping the city a finger.

Deciding to take the shortest way home, Maji walks up the street that cuts between two very distinct sections of his neighborhood: the Lamb and Melville Projects. Maji's family has called Melville home for three generations. Just up the block sits a small squat building with blue and gold crosses on the window that Maji was baptized in. Around the corner is his favorite bodega that was once a farmer's market, back when the Bronx was nothing but farmland.

Maji walks in between the two large buildings, feeling the coolness of their shadows pass over his arms and neck. When his dad was Maji's age, both buildings were known as Melville and made up one of the largest housing complexes in the Bronx. This was before the city split them on a map.

Compared to Melville's brown-bricked face and round shape, Lamb is a towering building with over fifty floors. One summer, when Maji was nine, there had been a blackout in the Bronx. Maji heard that a few older people couldn't get down from the top floors during the heatwave. The city didn't seem to give a damn—neighbors had to carry some down all twenty flights to save a few.

Some didn't make it.

Maji walks up three flights of stairs and notices that his neighbor's door is wedged open with a broom, probably to air out the heat from her cooking. This is standard practice in the Bronx: you keep your door open to flush out the heat and dry your clothes on the fire escape. Then, whatever extra space you can find, you use it.

As Maji turns the key to his apartment, he takes in the aroma of Senegalese dakhine and kandia.

Just past his door, Maji finds his mom at the stove making dinner. Her body is rocking back and forth while she mixes the steel pot with a large wooden spoon. Behind her, the speakers are blaring music. The sounds call her from her father's tongue, and she sings as if in conversation. Her eyes are closed. She smiles between every line and lyric.

For more reasons than he understands, seeing her like this brings warmth to Maji's neck and face.

When she spots him standing in the doorway, grinning like a maniac, Maji's mom wraps him in her arms and tries to dance with him. There was a time when he would laugh and giggle, trying to keep up with her. But now Maji is a whole foot taller than her, and he stumbles around. When he doesn't move, she sucks her teeth and goes back to cooking.

"What are you making?" he asks.

Instead of answering, she sings and sways. But with a little gesture, she points over to a cookbook.

Maji squints at the page and immediately gets smacked on the head. Maji's mom hip-checks him out of the kitchen, shouting after him to put his glasses on and clean his room before dinner.

While he finds his mother's good mood a little annoying, deep down inside, Maji also enjoys it. More than anyone else he knows, Maji can sense her emotions wash over him like a fog when she feels overwhelmed; like a chest full of fireworks when she was excited about an upcoming event. Even as he walks away, her slow, melodic music fills his body with electricity.

A part of Maji relates to the mood swings he sees in her. Sometimes you feel invincible—like your feet can glide over the pavement. And the next moment, you're underneath the concrete, under everyone in the city's stone slabs and rough heels. Maji has never told his mother that he can feel her this way. He slides his glasses off of the bookcase and puts them on. It's not a secret that he hates wearing them, even in the house. To him, wearing glasses just gives people reasons to think less of you. The Bronx is a place that's just looking for weakness, and Maji wasn't going to let it set its hooks into him.

His room is a mess, but it's the kind of mess he feels comfortable with—at home. As he finishes cleaning up (one sock over here … one pillow over there), he finds the book he's been reading for Mr. D's class on the floor. The book is leather-bound with gold-printed waves skimming across the cover. In the center is the head of a giant whale breaching the water and rising upward, mouth and teeth baring at the sky.

Just as he leaves his room, the door to his parent's bedroom is slightly open to see inside. His father is pulling the navy blue shirt over his large shoulders and tucking the bottom into his pants. No wonder his mother is in such a good mood, Maji thinks. His father was never home during the day.

Maji walks up to the door, and his father sees him in the mirror's reflection.

"Maji."

"Hey, Dad."

Out of all the people in his life, Maji doesn't have the same unique "connection" with his father. Maybe at some point he did, but that was so long ago that his memory is hazy. All of the warm colors and emotions Maji gets from reading his mom are gone when he looks at his dad. For Maji, trying to read his father's emotions is like trying to see into a slab on concrete.

He tries to form the words in his mouth, but his father cuts him off.

"How's school going?"

His back is still to Maji. He focuses more on his tie than what he says.

"It's fine."

"Good."

"Are you staying for dinner?"

Maji hates himself as soon as this question leaves his lips.

Over the last six months, Maji has sensed a change in their energy. He has never been able to explain where this intuition comes from, but Maji has learned to listen to them as they are whispers people don't want you to hear. The signs have been there for him, Maji: his parents were on the verge of splitting up. This came from the family that had spent their lives together in this little apartment. They used to have movie nights, sandwich-eating competitions, and some of the best Halloween costumes in the Bronx. But that was a lifetime ago.

Coupled with this, Maji and his father had drifted apart. Sometimes he will go days without even seeing him. Ever since he got into high school, the distance between him and his dad grew. Maji doesn't know how this divide started, but he knows what's played a significant factor.

"I have to work," his father says with a sigh. When he turns, Maji can see the sharp parts of his uniform: the nameplate and the badge. As he slips into his large belt, he clasps the walkie-talkie talk mic to his left shoulder. He gives a light tap to the gun in its holster to check that it's secure.

Maji steps aside as his dad brushes by him. Maji tries to meet eyes with him as he passes, but his father doesn't seem to see him.

After closing the door to his room, Maji sits on the floor and pulls the book onto his lap. Whatever joy he has left in him from the long day is gone, and he doesn't feel like eating dinner.

Maji's room shares a wall with the kitchen; through this, he hears muffled shouting. The colors of the argument seem to bleed through the painted walls in green and black trails—the smell of his parent's voices pangs in his nostrils like bitter coffee beans.

There's a loud slam of a door.

And his mom turns off the radio.

Chapter 4 ⌒

Ten days before Maji braved the waters of the Hudson . . .

Mr. D. walks around Maji's seat and climbs across the desk. He always takes this perch when Maji talks to him after class.

"So that's what you think? I'm interested in how you got to that conclusion without even finishing the book."

Flustered, Maji flips through the pages. "Ishmael has seen some crazy stuff up until this point, right? But that's why he went out to sea in the first place. His life was boring. He didn't have connections to anyone on land."

"And what about Ahab?"

"He's the same as Ishmael. They both have something to prove and it's out there, on the ocean."

Mr. D. rocks his head from side to side as if listening to music in the room's silence.

"You sound like you agree with them."

Maji closes the book. "Imagine what's going to happen when they catch that whale—and yes, I do think they'll catch it and it'll be my boy Ish who does it. Not Ahab. Watch! Take my word for it. And when he does, it's going to be like bringing a miracle home or something. Imagine how small everyone is going to feel. How small the world's going to be."

Maji catches a faint blue wisp of smoke that pours out of the man's nose. On his tongue, he can suddenly taste honey. Maji's odd sense sometimes fires off like this randomly, but he can tell that Mr. D is humored by his response.

"What is it?"

"It's just that your answer reminds me of something I read. It said that Melville was interested in the unknowable and the unreachable parts of our world."

Maji laughs. "How can you know the unknowable?"

"Exactly. The sea to him was the most mysterious and unreachable place in our world. Even now, we don't know what's at the bottom of the ocean. What you're saying is that both Ishmael and Ahab were drawn to the water by something they could not see. Do you think it's possible for a creature to have that power?"

Maji hesitates at first to answer. He wants to tell Mr. D about the strange emotions he can sense in people and their effect on him. He wants to tell him of the nightmare that seems to drag him out of his bed at night as if an invisible claw had a hold of his body.

"What if Ishmael *could* feel something out in the ocean."

Mr. D thinks about this for a second. "Like fate."

"More than fate. Like being called to something—or someone."

Maji isn't sure if he's taking the conversation too far, so he reads the man's face intently.

"That's interesting. You know it's said that what Melville was trying to write about was of the 'unknowable'—powers and forces that, like the ocean, are beyond our realm of knowledge."

"Like God?"

Mr. D's eyebrows pop up at this. "Ishmael is a religious name, after all."

"First son of Abraham."

Maji watches his teacher turn to him. "I wasn't aware you had a religious background, Maji."

To Maji, the comment feels like someone's splashed cold water on him. He stumbles to gather himself. "M-my mom used to go to church. My dad wanted me to go to Sunday School 'cause he went. . ."

Regretting going this far, Maji breaks eye contact with Mr. D. Almost as if on cue, the older man changes the subject. "I think you could be right, about Ishmael. But maybe

it's not like God at all. What you seem to be talking about
is a connection to the sea. As if Ishmael is being drawn
there. Humans are always looking for answers. And what
bigger or more mysterious question is there to answer
than what lies in the ocean? Ishmael doesn't understand
but *has* to see the unknowing himself. All rivers lead to the
sea, I guess."

Mr. D. looks at his watch and hops down from the
desk. "Speaking of which, I need to lead myself out of here.
I hope you give me more of that insight when the book's
done. And I hope you're not losing sleep reading, Maji. You
dozed off twice in my class. And I *know* I'm not boring."

Even though his voice sounds half joking, Maji recognizes that this question is Mr. D's gentle way of checking
in. While he's never brought it up, it's no secret that this
last school year has been rough for Maji—both in the
building and at home. A few fights back in September.
One in-school suspension to close out the fall. Maji even
missed one whole week of class just before Christmas
because his father didn't let him leave the house. This was
his punishment for running away one cold December
night.

Maji knows that if Mr. D. hadn't been there for him at
school, he wouldn't have finished this year. He may have
never gone back to school, period.

Part of him wants to tell his favorite teacher why he's
been staying up to read. About the cold flashes. About the
nightmare. Part of him trusts Mr. D. more than anyone in

the world. But then Maji hears the whisper of doubt again. Never look weak. *Never.*

"I'm good."

With a careful glance, Mr. D. then nods. "Then go. Try all things and achieve what you can," he loudly shouts while closing his leather bag with one hand and shoving Maji out of the door with the other.

That night, Maji wakes up from his nightmare and pulls his legs over the side of his bed. There's so much sweat on his neck and face that he might have come out of the ocean.

He flicks on his phone.

It only takes a few seconds into the video for him to know that C2.0 isn't his usual crazy self. One arm lays flat on his desk. The other is propping his head up. The boy's eyes are looking directly at the camera. His hair, usually nicely braided, is out on one side, and he isn't wearing a shirt.

This isn't anything new. In the three years C.20 has been streaming, Maji has stuck with him through the vlogger's ups and downs. It isn't always dumb vids and silly dances. Sometimes he got honest about his feelings and struggles. For example, that one time, his mother got sick and was hospitalized. Or he had to take some time off from his channel when there was a fire in his building. While some say this was him drumming up drama for clicks, Maji doesn't care. He knows that there is nobody more real than Consciousness 2.0.

But not tonight. Instead, the boy's eyes seem dead as he speaks.

"A short one today, C2.0 Nation. I just figured I'd give y'all an update. Been losing sleep recently. Didn't get no sleep after yesterday's nonsense, but I wanted to address a few things. So here it is."

Maji can't help but feel like something is off, but he keeps watching.

"I can deal with haters. Haters, you can come find me. I'm not hiding. You can come find me. But . . ." C2.0 stops himself and shakes his head. He stands and begins yelling. "Fuck it. Like I'm going to let you all knock me down? Like I'm going to let you get to me?" He pounds his chest with his fist over and over. He strikes himself so hard that, after a while, the blows leave bruised imprints on his skin. He then looks directly into the camera and laughs. "C2.0 and the C2.0 Nation is for life. Ain't no way we stopping now. I am untouchable! We are eternal." He flashes his trademark sign-off and seems bursting with life as the screen goes black.

Maji turns his screen over onto his pillow and takes a deep breath. After a weird start to the video, part of him feels better seeing C2.0 stand up for himself. He's not sure what happened, but at least he isn't going to roll over for anyone.

As he lies in the dark, the nightmare haunting him for

the last week rushes over him like black water. He's below the surface again, drowning. And in the recesses of this darkness, he feels something stirring—a large, powerful creature.

Whatever this feeling is, Maji struggles to give it a name. He takes another breath, but it feels hot in his lungs. He can't place it, but it scares him. Finally, he sets his feet flat on the cold floor, and the rocking stops. It's like gravity remembers his body. Only when the world finally returns is Maji able to take a breath.

As his senses return to normal, a word crawls into his mind. It's not one Maji's ever used, and he's unsure where he learned it. But this is the type of word you feel before you can understand. A sensation that makes his limbs heavy and his mouth dry. It bubbles to the surface in more ways than one.

Dread.

Maji feels dread.

Chapter 5 ᓆ

Nine days before Maji went to face the ocean alone . . .

THE phone feels as heavy as a stone in Maji's hand as he stares at the screen.

The video is only two minutes and thirty-two seconds long.

By Wednesday morning, the video already has 3.7 million views.

The woman is dark-skinned and is wearing her black hair up. She has her back to the camera as someone records her from a phone. She is wearing a tan skirt, a white tank top, and a bookbag contorted on her back, one strap hanging down, slapping her hip as she walks. Her arms are curled around her chest as if carrying a heavy load.

She is laughing with whoever is holding the camera.

When the cops first appear onscreen, the smile slips her face, and the laughing stops. She tries walking by them. At first, it doesn't seem like they are there for her. But as soon as one cop pulls out his sidearm and the second one follows suit, there is this fear in her eyes. Whoever is recording her shouts,

"Hey! Hey!" and he gets closer. His voice is loud and angry. "What's wrong? Hey!"

One officer spins his gun on the man recording and shouts for him to back up.

"I'm not doing shit," the man yells. "That's my wife and son. What are you doing to them?"

The other cop is telling the woman to put her hands up.

"I'm holding my baby. I can't put my hands up. I'm holding my baby," she screams over and over.

With one arm still aiming his weapon, the officer reaches over and begins wrenching the bookbag off the woman's back.

"Yo. Get your hands off my wife! You're going to drop my son."

The second officer pushes the camera away as he tries to advance, claiming she has stolen that bag from a CVS and that it was all caught on video.

The woman isn't trying to resist. She's just trying to keep her footing and not let the baby fall from her grasp. Finally, the officer pulls with so much force that the woman nearly falls. She's trying to stay upright. There is yelling. Her husband tries to push through to reach her. The sound of a shot, a scream, a baby crying, and an officer's blaring radio making no sense.

The screen faces the blue sky.

With his hand trembling under the weight, Maji turns off his screen.

The video is only two minutes and thirty-two seconds long.

By Wednesday evening, the video already has 12.1 million views.

Chapter 6 ⌒

Eight days before Maji ventured out into the cold water . . .

THE first protest in New York happens quickly. Unlike the Florida shooting (which occurred just last week), the reaction to the video coming out of Chicago is fast. Organizers spring up on every platform and every possible newsfeed overnight. Even Maji, who stays away from political circles (mainly because they feel a thousand miles outside of his body), can't avoid the images of people walking down Broadway by the hundreds.

The signs.

The chants.

That night, the police showed up to a peaceful protest in Washington Square Park and fired pepper spray and smoke into the crowd. A car is set on fire. Broken glass is everywhere. The next day, the mayor calls for all schools to be closed "for the safety of the public."

A curfew is set in New York: no one out after 8 P.M. unless it's an emergency.

The second night of protests is worse than the first.

To Maji, hearing about protests in New York is like a movie. They march down from Harlem to Lower Manhattan. They lock down points in Brooklyn. There are even a few in The Bronx. On social media, Maji scrolls through pictures of his friends with their fists in the air, mouths open in mid-chant.

Maji stays away from the protests. He knows quite a few of his friends from school that are just posers—taking selfies and acting all "woke" when they aren't. While he agrees that what happened to that woman on the video is terrible, Maji has never liked the idea of crowds and knows that his mom would lose her mind if she knew that he had gone to a protest.

Maji doesn't even want to know what his father would say if he caught him at one. In his mind, he was more likely to see his father there than at home.

As Maji steps off of the train that afternoon, his body moves as if his joints are rusted over. With the nightmare draining him of his sleep every night and the constant line of bad news on his feeds, Maji is on autopilot. He hasn't had the time or energy to read—he's already behind on his schoolwork. A numbness has set into his interactions with the world that makes everything seem alien. Like he's lost the language to understand.

Part of him wants to think that all of this is going to pass. Eventually, his life will start making sense again.

But why does this feel different?

Maji rounds the corner to Melville, his thumb swiping past one block of anxiety after another on his phone. Right as he's about to push the main door open, Maji finds himself standing in front of his father.

A sudden anxiety wraps Maji's chest like a fever. He feels trapped in this moment. While he can feel his father's gaze on him, Maji's own eyes can't pull away from the boxes this man is hauling—the arm of a hastily stuffed shirt hanging idly out of one of the bent lids; the stuffed book bag slung over the man's shoulder.

"You ... school?" he asks. These are the only two words Maji understands. They sound garbled in Maji's ears.

Before he can react, Maji's father takes his phone right out of his hand and looks at the screen. Maji had accidentally left a video playing of one of the protests.

There was a time he cared about it. There was a time his mom and dad used to talk about the people dying in the streets. But as soon as Maji got into high school, those talks stopped. He wasn't sure why. The recent shootings made everything a minefield.

Maji's father closes the video and tosses the phone back.

"I don't want to see you anywhere near that, you hear me?" he yells as he turns and walks away.

Faint prickles of heat run down Maji's back and neck. The blood is rushing to his face. His fathers was walking away from him *again*. Leaving *again*. Treating him as if he was still five-years-old and needed his protection. As the rage blooms up from his chest like a cloud of heat, Maji shouts,

"I'm not a kid anymore! I can go where I want!"

At first Maji thinks that his father hasn't heard him, but then he spins around and is right in Maji's face. It happens so fast that Maji's whole body tenses up to defend itself.

"This ain't a discussion," his father tells him through clenched teeth. "I said that I want you to stay out of this. Get home and stay put."

Maji feels the swell of anger burning in his chest and steps closer. He wants to lash out at him. He wants to yell. Everything this man used to be—loving, careful, thought-ful—it's like that man is dead. What's left behind is a tyrant: a man who treats Maji like he probably treats every other black boy on the street when he's in uniform. How can he be this man's son when he only feels like his enemy?

Maji feels the word *hate* forming on his tongue. But just as it's about to leave his lips, the anger quickly vanishes when he reads the wild look in this man's eyes. This look is obvious.

It's Maji's eyes when Ms. Finn kicked him out of her class.

48

It's his eyes when people stand too close on the subway.

With Maji's own anger gone, a deep fear falls into that space inside of him instead.

"Dad?"

As if recognizing this tone in Maji's voice, his father backs off. Maji tries to read him, but it's like looking at a blank wall. He used to have a connection with his father, the same he has with his mom. But now Maji has gone blind. What is he feeling right now? Fear? Shame?

With nothing left to say, his father turns and walks away.

But for Maji, he knows now where the rage he sometimes feels comes from.

It's in his blood.

Chapter 7 ⌒

Seven days before the ocean swallowed up a young boy . . .

THE phone buzzes in Maji's hand, and the shock nearly makes him spill out of bed.

He squints at the screen. It is 2 A.M., and he realizes he has fallen asleep watching YouTube again. He sees that it's a message from Crespo.

It's all over

Maji writes, ?
What's all over???

U good??? U didn't hear???

Maji swipes the screen. His first thought was that another protest had gone wrong, and the city had worsened. But he can't find anything. So finally, Crespo sends him three links, back-to-back-to-back.

The first link takes too long to load, so Maji clicks the second, sending him to a familiar place. Consciousness 2.0's newest video was posted just fourteen hours prior. Maji quickly throws his earbuds in, thinking that C2.0 is stirring up his usual internet beef again. He restarts the video and huddles over the screen.

"Sup C2.0 Nation. This one's going to be a short video, mainly cause it's going to be my last."

Maji sits up. *Is he shutting down his channel?* The first thing to cross his mind is that C2.0 is in one of his moods. He loves to get under people's skin. But the guy doesn't look right. For one, he isn't in his usual room. He is high up somewhere, looking out at the city. The sun is just coming up.

"I know I'm not a good person," he says directly to the camera, which he holds in his hand. "I treated a lot of people like shit, so they treated me like shit. But, of course, what goes around comes around and all that. I'm man enough to admit I deserved it."

His face is so pale. His eyes are distant. He seems off.

Maji minimizes the video and flips to the last link, whose web address he recognizes as C2.o's social media profile, but it comes back as "Page Not Found."

Can't believe this shit. My sis is crying. She loved him.

To Maji, this is an odd thing for Crespo to say. Sure, his channel was popular, and he has fans, but streamers come and go. He's sure C2.o is just taking a break. He'd be back.

As if in response to this thought, C2.o, still speaking from the available video on the other page, says,

"I can't . . . ."

He shakes his head and looks down as if thinking his words over. Then, he puts the camera down and walks away.

Maji will never forget the way the sunrise looks in that sky.

The way the red and yellow drink the darkness from the clouds.

There's nothing else. Nothing but a blooming sky for a few minutes, and then C2.o leans down and turns off the video. He uploaded it just like that.

Maji's jaw is locked. Anxiety is surging its way up to his neck and throat. He clicks over to the first link.

BODY OF 19-YEAR-OLD VLOGGER
FOUND AFTER CRYPTIC POST

Maji sets the phone down because his hands are cold and numb. He rubs them together and tries his best to scroll. But unfortunately, it feels like someone is hammering nails into his fingertips whenever he touches the screen. Maji's eyes skim the words so fast that they aren't all registering.

Friends were worried . . .
Neighbors found the body of Damien Greene, also known as Consciousness 2.0 . . .
. . . jumped from the roof of a ten-story apartment building . . .

Maji's breath becomes thin and ragged as the room rocks back and forth. He can hear the walls creaking, and the shadows cast on the wall from the tree outside seem to spin along with the groaning. His nightmare is alive and reaching out for him.

As the phone falls from his hand, the video skims back to the last few seconds. And he hears the boy's last words.

"I can't. . . ."

Chapter 8 ⌐

Five days before Maji went out to find a miracle on the vast ocean . . .

HE uses the bathroom and gets dressed, moving silently through the motions. The numbness Maji has been feeling for the last few days is now spread into his emotions. While his heart isn't into going to school, it's the last day of the school year. It's 6 A.M., and it seems like the entire building—the entire world—is asleep. The only hint of light sneaks in from the blinds. Maji unplugs his phone, pockets his train pass, shoulders his bookbag, and leaves his room.

He walks by the bookcase where his glasses are perched and pushes his mother's bedroom door open to say good-bye. Instead of being asleep, he finds her sitting up in her bed, pillows propped against the wall behind her. Her lower half is covered in sheets. She has no expression on her face. Instead, her eyes are wide open.

"Bye, mom."

She blinks. Her chest rises and falls, but she doesn't see him.

Maji quietly closes the door, though he keeps his eyes on her until she vanishes.

Chapter 9 ⁓

Five days before Maji saw his first ocean sunrise . . .

AFTER getting his late pass, Maji breaks into a full sprint down the hallway. A rail fire on the D line had made him thirty minutes late. Usually, he wouldn't give a damn about making it to class on time. But this was his last English class of the year. On his train ride, Maji had mustered up the energy to finish the book. He felt like the last few pages had lit a fire in his belly, and for the first time in a long time, felt in control of something. He now knew what he wanted to tell Mr. D: about Ishmael and Ahab, about the miracle out in the sea.

He runs with the book tucked under his arm.

As soon as he gets through the door, Maji makes his way to his desk. The classroom is dead quiet as the students watch him as he works his way to the back. Mr. D is sitting at his desk, the leg of his glasses clenched between his teeth as if he is in the middle of saying something important.

It was like no one wanted to make a sound.

"I told the class, Maji, that I won't be coming back next year."

Maji searches his teacher's face for the rest. The joke. The punchline.

There's a long pause.

Maji watches as Mr. D's eyes turn away.

"I'm sorry I'm breaking this to you all on the last day of school, but I didn't want to distract us from your final projects. And I only say this now because everything I've taught you in this class about reading and writing—you know I care about it. It's all important. But what I value more than anything is that you all know how to use those skills to stand up for yourselves. That you're well-informed about what's happening in this world. You all have to go past this block, past this neighborhood. I'm going to be honest—it's crazy out there. The shootings, the protests. I want all of you to use your heads out there. Even if all you do is write stories or songs or poems. Even if all you do is open up a corner store and hold that down. As long as it's moving us away from where we are now, I know I did my job."

Mr. D speaks some more, allowing students to react to

the news, but most of it roars like static in Maji's brain.

White noise. He feels dizzy.

Maji stands with the rest of the students at the end of class to walk out. But instead of moving towards the door, his legs feel heavy. He throws his hood over his head just as the warm tears stream down his face. Maji can't remember the last time he cried. Maybe as a toddler?

Afraid to move and have his classmates see, Maji stands there. Picking up on this, Mr. D asks to clear the class of stragglers. When everyone is gone, he takes his glasses off and approaches him.

"I'm sorry this is happening." His voice is low and calm, but it doesn't make Maji feel any better. Instead, the tears shake loose and drip down his cheek and neck.

"I want you to graduate, Maji. I want to see you getting out of here and getting out in the world to do whatever you can do. You're smart, man. You're a bonehead most of the time, but you're also creative like all-hell. You set your mind to things and just get it done. You work harder than anyone else in this class. Just keep it up. You understand what I'm telling you?"

Maji wipes his face with his sleeve. Before he can realize what he's saying, the words spill from his lips.

"I can't . . . ."

"Maji—"

"I can't be here." He shakes his head as the static scrapes away at his ears. "You're the best teacher I ever had. And now you're just leaving? Just like that? You're just gone?"

Mr. D sets a hand on his shoulder, but Maji's body is numb, and he can't feel the weight of it. "I got something for you. It's in my office. Let me go and pick it up, and we can talk about this. I'm not leaving any time soon. We can talk about college recommendations, I promise. Give me five, no, three minutes. I'll be right back. Don't you move."

As soon as he disappears through the door, Maji waits until it closes before grabbing his bag and flipping the strap over one shoulder. He's shaking so much that he's about to break apart. To Maji, the revelation feels like it's ripped a gaping void in his chest; an endless vacuum of empty space. Now graduation seems useless.

Now the world waiting for him after high school seems vast and impossible—like the nightmare that's been haunting him every night. The police shootings, C2.0's suicide, his home. Everything feels like it's crumbling underneath his feet and he's drowning. Even the walls of the room feel as if they are caving in at the dark edges of his sight line.

Gasping.

The tears cool on his cheeks as his body grows hotter than a fever. Red flashes explode across his vision. Wanting to let this fire out of his skin before it boils him alive, Maji sweeps everything off of Mr. D's desk. Books, pencils, and papers spill onto the ground.

Still shaking, Maji thinks about slamming the leather-bound book to the ground. But instead, he shoves the tome into his book bag and runs out of the room.

An alarm goes off when he slams his shoulder into the

outside door. Maji doesn't stop running until he's already on the train platform, watching the next train pull in. Maji's head swims, and he feels dizzy. Sweat pools around his legs and arms. He feels like he's floating, like a lost balloon, floating out with no anchor.

He can't breathe.
He feels sluggish.
He wants to throw up.

Maji can't tell what train he's on, but it doesn't matter. The stress feels like it's overloading his brain, and he wants to close his eyes.
And he does.

Sometime later, Maji feels a hot wind blow over his face, and he wakes to see that the train doors are open. He isn't sure how long he's been out, but he also doesn't recognize the name of the train stop except for the part that says "Coney Island."

As if on invisible strings, Maji feels his body stand, recovers his bookbag, and stumbles onto the platform. All of Maji's senses are on fire. The air tastes prickly—his ears rattle. The edges of his skin seem to sag on the edges as if gravity is about to tear him in half.

Maji walks for blocks under this stress, shielding his eyes and ears to gather himself. His body aches as if someone has slammed hammers into his joints. His stomach feels full of rot. And yet, his feet still carry him to the largest structure in the distance.

The rides in Coney Island are on, but no one is riding them. The Ferris wheel, the rollercoaster: there is a smoothness to the way they spill through the air. As if watching their spinning lights and infectious music rekindles a memory in him, Maji remembers that his father was supposed to bring him here for his last birthday. The thought forms a sour patch in his mouth.

In the distance, the ghostly trails of sounds appear in Maji's eyes. And almost on their own, his feet carry him past the amusement park's glittering lights.

The soft cry of seagulls and the rush of water slapping against the shore appear like pale blues and greens, tendrils from another world. From the boardwalk, the ocean looks endless. It's a hot day, and the sun reflects off the sand and water in a way that makes Maji squint.

The crashing waves vibrate against Maji's ribcage and lungs. The rise and fall of sound set pinpricks into his arms and legs. He realizes this feeling is like his nightmare, but instead of fear, Maji is suddenly filled with a longing for feeling the water on his skin, the ocean bounding endlessly in the distance, and the wind in his face.

He's lost so much: his past, his present. No family. No school. The only thing Maji can see in his future now is death; another black body for "thoughts and prayers" and picket signs.

But what if there is something else?

Maji strains his eyes to look at the water's edge, just under the burning sun.

And he sees something.

A shadow rises out of the surface and then disappears again.

Maji can feel the straps of his bookbag biting into his fingers as if the book inside is stirring. In his mind, he can hear his teacher's voice again.

. . . *Melville was trying to write about the 'unknowable'—powers and forces that, like the ocean, are beyond our realm of knowledge. Ishmael is connected to the sea. And even though he doesn't understand it, he's drawn to her. It's like they say— all rivers lead to the sea.*

Maji feels the call.

The call of a miracle.

Part 2 ~~~
The Sea

Chapter 10 ⌒

MAJI spends his first full day on the ocean, checking between his map and phone. There is no service out here, but there are times that his location blips into existence. Of course, there's no way to tell if this is accurate, but with the city of New York behind him and nothing but the sprawl of the same ocean reaching in every direction, Maji notes it on his fold-out map. By his estimate, he had sailed out of the Lower Bay and was just now drifting into the start of the Atlantic.

Maji sticks to his schedule and puts into play everything he's read. Setting up his makeshift mast (ten-inch steel pipes lashed into a cross), he binds the blankets around the edges in hopes of catching the wind. Unfortunately, it doesn't work as well as he had hoped and slumps over. With such a small sail, the difference in speed over the water is unnoticeable. Luckily the current seems to be doing most of the work, with every wave thrusting the raft forward.

The two blue drums Maji had stolen from the recycling warehouse back in Melrose are keeping the raft afloat nicely. With them tied to both sides of the raft, he only needs to worry about keeping the front and back from taking in too much water. Two inflatable tubes keep both ends from dipping too far beneath the surface, and the wooden platforms bound in rain tarps (used in the same warehouse by its forklifts) provide enough of a floor to keep the whole thing—for the most part—in one piece. Finally, the entire jalopy was held together with knots he had practiced over and over for days until his hands hurt. Most of it is now in his muscle memory.

While building the ship, Maji knew that with his raft only being roughly ten feet by ten, he had two things he had to make sure to look out for: large waves that could tip him into the water, and that the seawater stayed on the outside of the boat. From what he's read, the two primary laws of the ocean are don't drink the saltwater and keep dry.

The day is overcast, with thick, billowing clouds stretching as far as Maji's eyes can follow. The June heat sits around his chest and shoulders, but the seawater splashes cold and frothy. The wind kicks up behind his tiny sail and rattles the mast. All the while, Maji keeps his eyes around him at all times.

Luckily, when the daylight fades and the night curls over the scope of the sea, the fear of being spotted by either planes or passing ships falls away. If that were to happen, Maji knows that he and his little, soggy raft will be powerless to resist being taken away.

As the moon blossoms above his head, Maji stares at the hundreds of stars joining it to light the night sky. Maji has never seen so many stars in his life. He never knew so many existed.

Maji sets his phone on the floor of the raft and checks on the knots of the boat as the tiny speakers blare Aaron May's "Let Go." The water around the boat is a beautiful emerald green and the waves seem to be dancing toward the light of the moon. He feels that each dark wave that curls alongside the boat makes music against the wood.

He takes a breath and lies cross-legged, looking up at the stars. They shine so vividly that when he reaches up with his hand, Maji feels close enough to pluck a shining gem down for himself as if tearing it from a piece of fabric.

Maji laughs to himself, and then this laughter escapes his lips and lifts to the night sky. At one point, there was a life he had been living—a life governed by rules that he could never understand. When to speak. When to speak up. Keep your head up, boy. Keep your head down. Run, walk, slow down, speed up. And the moment he broke one of those rules, he could end up dead. Hell, he could die for following every single one of them. The world on land didn't make sense.

But Maji looks out on the ocean and realizes that *this*, more than any experience in his life, makes the most sense. On the ocean, *he* is in control. There's nothing complex about the water around him. Nothing unfair about what she gives and what she takes away. Out here, there are no YouTube followers and protests and college applications and overdue bills. No silences between loved ones.

Nothing but Maji and the miracle he knows is out there waiting for him.

Chapter 11 ⌐

B Y the second day, Maji realizes that the sun is the first major problem he has to contend with. Without cloud cover, the afternoon heat eats away at his skin. It's an odd combination of things. Maji had thought, after his first two days, that with the saltwater constantly splashing against the side of the raft, he would feel cool. But the ocean is a shifting mirror reflecting the heat. It is worse today than Maji had ever expected. Its rays put weight onto his bones; burns patches of rough skin on his neck and forehead. There's no running from the piercing light, either. Maji wants to strip naked *and* somehow keep covered at the same time.

In the late afternoon, the waves grow bigger than Maji has ever seen. Maji fights against them for two hours until things calm down. Once or twice, his foot slips into the cold ocean water sending a jet of ice into his veins. Most of the pain shoots up through his hands as the saltwater eats the rope burns in his palms.

Maji scowls at the sunset on the third day. While it was his toughest day so far, he sits down and chuckles to himself. *It's going to take a lot more than that to make me turn around.*

He snacks on chips and cookies to keep his calorie intake high as the sun vanishes. He drinks water sparingly. Maji's packed five gallons of water, as much as he could carry, but he knows better than to go over the limit. He has no idea what rationing food looks like, but in his mind, he's packed enough for at least a seven-day trip.

As if in competition with his day, Maji can immediately tell that the night wasn't going to be an easy one. While it's removed the torture of the sun's rays, a sharp wind spins over the surface of the sea. At first, Maji's grateful. He welcomes the way this wind catches his sail. But the gusts of air turn into a sustained howling that nearly rips out the lashed wooden pillar at the center of his raft. Maji feels as if the wind is slamming into the sea, skimming the surface, and then rebounds back into the sky. Angered, the waves go from a deep emerald to a dark blue as they expand and crash. With this, the temperature drops down to the point where Maji feels like he's about to freeze to death. Luckily, he's packed a warm sweater, something that seemed dumb to him at first but now seems like a godsend.

Light is also a significant issue during the night. Maji tries using his cellphone, but there's only so much a tiny screen can illuminate. With nothing on the horizon, the moon does all it can to make things somewhat visible. And yet, to Maji, the ocean runs on endlessly and vanishes into a blackness that is ready to swallow him whole. As they rock the tiny raft back and forth, Maji tries his best to lean on one end of the raft, forcing the balance with his body while also making sure his food and storage (not to mention himself) don't go flying off the boat and into the waiting mouth of the ocean.

When the next day comes into full view, the sun returns to lashing his arms and back. Maji uses the blankets from the sail to make a mini fort and protect himself. The extra layers at least shield him from the sun's rays which seem to sink into him like knives.

Before a dull sensation of regret spills over him, before the thought of his mom creeps into his mind, Maji pops his earbuds in and goes into his bag. He pulls out the leather-bound book with the gold-laced cover and begins to read.

There's no turning back now.

Maji has faith.

What else does he have?

Chapter 12 ⌐

WATER.

    It's the entire world. It's the horizon. It's the shifting surface below Maji's boat.

On this fourth day out on the sea, the water sounds different to Maji. During the day, the waves lap against his raft in a sweeping pattern—a powerful form of violence. The tiny raft bobs up and down as the water hisses, claps, and roars. At night, the moon makes the waves hiss and foam. The warning of a threat.

The sun and the ocean: these all-powerful things that Maji had taken for granted living in a small two-bedroom apartment in the Bronx. He had first seen the freedom of the sea as something that he could adapt to his own thinking. Now, rocking on its surface, Maji realizes that the sea doesn't care for him; the ocean doesn't need him. The moment it decides, the water will roll over and crush him flat—wipe him out instantly. There have been times in his life when Maji has felt small and insignificant. And yet the more that he's out on the water, this powerlessness grows inside him.

A quote comes to Maji's mind like a ghost whispering into his ear.

"Noah's flood has not yet subsided."

The waves around him carry a musicality to them—a call and response rising from the ocean that reminds Maji of the trembling voices in a church. Maji remembers the old church his mom and dad used to frequent. The organ would play so damn loud, you could hear it down the block. During the summer, when the doors needed to be propped open because the congregation's AC was on the fritz, it was like you were getting a curbside sermon every Sunday.

Maji shakes his head as if his body is caught in the web of this memory.

He looks out at the moon as it summons ghostly trails on the surface of the water.

That night, while lying flat on his back and looking at the pictures on his phone (mostly of his mother), Maji spots an ant crawling along the edge of his fingers. He marvels at this little stowaway and wonders to himself.

Does he know how small he is?
Does he know how big this ocean is?
Does he care?

～ ～ ～

On his sixth sunset on the ocean, Maji hears something out in the water. Typically the waves rock up and down a little stronger at night than during the day, but nothing unusual.

But the sound he hears is something else.

No waves rushing.

Not the ocean doing what the ocean does.

The sky is not yet clear of the day's sunlight for stars, and the moon is out but not entirely in place. Maji's vision is foggy as it's caught between the struggle of night and day.

And then he hears it again.

It is a low, booming sound followed by water splashing.

As he grips the edge of the raft, Maji peers out into the dark water.

The movement is very far out, maybe over a hundred yards away. The bulk is on the cusp of darkness, barely caught by moonlight. But Maji is sure that it's there.

A circle forms in a section of the ocean where the waves are not rising and falling. A white mass breaks through the surface.

From a distance, Maji can see something solid come out of the water; not all the way, but its skin is bright enough to distinguish it from the rippling, black ocean. Whatever it is, is massive, like an entire chunk of land rising out of the depths.

Though his raft is rocking hard enough to buck him off, Maji stands motionless, observing whatever has come to greet the moon.

Before he can steer towards it, a large sound erupts from the surface-unlike anything he's ever heard. The pulse is so deep and loud that it sends tremors through the ocean that leap into his boat. The tiny cracks and snaps from the sound alone threaten to tear the small raft in half, but Maji takes action. He dips his makeshift paddle in and tries to steer in the direction of the sound. But instead, he finds that the vibrations are causing the entire ocean to tremble, making his strokes mean nothing.

This is why I'm here.
This is what I came to see.
The miracle that will change the world is right in front of me.

Without a second thought, Maji jumps into the ocean. The blast of freezing water makes his chest seize, but he fights through the shock and tries to swim toward his destiny.

At that moment, Maji realizes that swimming is more complicated than it seems. His father had taught him the essentials of staying afloat and moving forward, but it's not like he often went to the pool or the beach to keep in practice. So as he hits the water, Maji splashes more than swims. He sweeps his arms. He chops at the water. But by the end, he looks back and has only made it five feet from the raft.

Maji shouts and waves his arms to get its attention, but he ends up sinking.

Another loud bellow shakes the entire ocean. Now submerged, Maji feels the water quake around him. It's so loud that he wants to slap his hands over his ears, but he's afraid of sinking to the bottom of the Atlantic.

Maji returns to the surface in time to see a jet of water shoot hundreds of miles into the sky. Then, as if summoned, gray clouds form and roll. The cover is so thick that it swallows up the stars and moon-like smoke trapped in a black bowl. In seconds, Maji stares at the eye of a massive storm.

Maji paddles back to the raft and pulls himself up, sprawling out onto the floor of the small boat. His clothes feel like they weigh a hundred pounds, and he can barely pick up his head. The wind is howling, and the sea roars with every loud wave crash.

A streak of lightning cuts a jagged arc and touches down against the ocean. As a sheet of heavy rain begins to fall from the sky, the waves heave upward like walls. Five feet. Six feet. A gust of wild wind rips the raft's makeshift mast and tosses it into the air.

Maji had been ready to face storms, but not one that would come so suddenly.

Something called down the storm.

This thought breaks when another rumble of thunder shakes the earth. Maji goes to work securing the raft, even while the ocean around him turns from a passive deep blue to foaming white-crested waves. With his bag of food and water already tied down, Maji scurries over and drops his book and cell phone in the plastic sandwich bags he uses to keep them dry. He then quickly grabs a loose rope and binds his wrists to the front of the raft. It's not something he's planned or practiced, but he works on instinct.

The first wave crashes into the front of the raft just as soon as the knot slips into place. The force alone sends the entire raft into the air. The impact tosses one of the floating drums into the sea, allowing the wind to finish turning the raft inside out.

A second barrel, still bound to the broken raft by a rope, is flung into the air. Maji drops down in time as it nearly beheads him. The force folds the entire raft onto itself, crushing Maji between this jagged edge and the floor.

Maji's ears are ringing, and his entire body is in pain. The back of his head struck one of the beams. But one specific part, the outer section of his thigh, is wildly shrieking in pain. Though it's submerged in saltwater, blood is pooling on the surface. With whatever strength he has left, he drags this limb from the ocean only to see a shard of wood the size of his hand embedded through his jeans.

Maji tries to scream, but seawater leaps into his mouth. He's barely hanging on. Barely alive. He came out to the sea to find magic. To find something to make sense of the world. But now he is hurting and lost. The only reason he is still alive rests in a last-minute knot he tied around his hand, which is now also bleeding profusely.

The blow to the head has spread numbness down Maji's neck and shoulders. He starts to feel light-headed. However, he can't explain why he wants to sleep. Everything is telling him to rest, but Maji forces his eyes open. Only partial thoughts survive in his head as the waves suck on his wound like a wet mouth. The knot around his wrist is loosening, and he is slipping into the sea. Around him . . .

. . . . the ocean still rolls like a beast awakened and hungry, but it's dying now.

. . . growing silent.

. . . the world is getting darker.

. . . eyes are so heavy . . .

. . . the storm is gone, but so is everything else.

Without intending to, and with the storm around him growing muted, Maji closes his eyes.

Chapter 13 ⌐

THE splash of water on his face startles Maji awake.
Where . . .

Thinking makes his head hurt.

His eyes are hazy, and he blinks to get them into focus. When they finally do, he thinks that his room looks barren. His bed is gone; he's sleeping on the floor.

Where am I?

As the realization sets in, Maji nearly calls for his mom. He wants to know she's near. He wants to press himself against her until he is consumed by her beating heart and soft music.

But Maji is not in his room, not in his apartment. Instead, he's floating on a single barrel lashed to a broken stump of wood. He is still in the middle of the ocean, hurting and cold, still hanging on by a knot.

Around him now sits the thickest fog Maji has ever seen. It hangs over the water like a curtain wide enough to block the sky.

Splashing.

Maji is so tired that he doesn't have the strength to cry out and ask what's there. Instead, his voice stops in his throat. His head is pounding. Every ounce of energy is gone.

The sound is getting louder. Whatever is in the fog is coming closer.

The only thing spared is the book with the black cover. Maji tries to grab it, but his body isn't listening to what he wants—a mixture of pain and fear.

The sound draws closer.

Maji looks in that direction.

Two white-hot eyes break through the fog and hang over him.

Maji feels lost in his thoughts again. The mist seems to seep into his ears, mouth, and nose. The eyes are a few feet away now.

Maji's own eyes are heavy again.

It's too soon. This isn't over. I should have lasted longer than this. I need to see, Maji tells himself. *I need to see it.*

Maji's body goes slack. The knot on his wrist opens, slipping him into the heart of the Atlantic.

And then he hears someone,

"Somebody get a lifeboat out here! There's someone in the water."

Chapter 14 ⤳

MAJI only remembers a few patches here and there. One second he's underwater, feeling the silence of the ocean pull him closer and closer to the darkness.

The next, he's being pulled upward. Someone has him by his waist and is gripping him tightly. For some reason, Maji thinks it's his dad. He's not sure why his mind leaps to this. Out of all places, why would his father be here?

The next few things Maji sees aren't real. He knows this but can't help himself. He sees the ocean and the tiny ship. He floats in closer and sees a boy smiling and taking in the sun.

The boy fears the moon, which is out alongside the sun. It's so big that you can count the craters.

Mr. DaCosta once told him—in the ways that Mr. D. knew random things in random ways—that the moon has an ocean on it. Not an actual one, but something called an ocean. Maji can't remember its name, but in this dream, he's afraid of the two seas colliding and drowning the world.

Maji spots something in the distance. It is as large as a ship and is leaping out of the water. It defies gravity. It lifts upward like a white cloud going to heaven. But then it gets too high, and Maji yells for it to be careful. The creature collides with the moon, and the rock cracks open like an egg, spilling green water into the blue ocean.

Screaming, Maji sits up and finds himself in a cot. His head hurts something awful, and his sightline swings back and forth as if he's still bobbing on the ocean. The room he's in is just a bit larger than his room in his own home. A few charts hang up on the walls, and books and binders lie in a bookcase. There is a small stove and fridge on the other side of the room.

Maji tries to move, but every inch of him is sore. His leg is exceptionally stiff, and he's in his underwear when he pulls the covers aside. Maji finds his leg wrapped in thick, white bandages. Though the wooden piece is gone, the pain calls right up from the bone.

A man Maji doesn't recognize is sitting by the wall with the books. His red hair is messy. His glasses hang desperately off his nose as he peers into a laptop. Hearing Maji stir, the two lock eyes. Then he jumps up and puts his hands up.

"You're okay. I promise. You're safe."

Realizing that he's almost naked, Maji covers himself quickly.

"You were wet," he says in a thick accent Maji can't place. "We had to get you out of your clothes or you would catch hypothermia." And then the man adds, "Just wait. Just wait."

He hurries over to the door and pulls it open, quickly calling for help. Two men appear instantly and join him in the room. The first is so tall that he has to stoop through the doorway. He is bald and has a thick, brown beard, but Maji can tell by his full cheeks that he's smiling. The second guy is pale and sickly, with big, poofy, purple bags underneath his eyes. He isn't smiling.

Realizing he's in trouble, Maji tries to get up to protect himself. *If these freaks get any closer . . .*

One last man comes through the door.

He has a thin mustache and soft eyes. He's bald and short in stature but broad along the shoulders. He reminds Maji of the men from his block. He is the kind of guy that, even in his thirties or forties, his smooth features and baby face lets him get away with looking like a teenager. The fact that he is black immediately glares among the other white faces.

This man glances between Maji and the men.

"Alright. Give him some air, man. Probably creeping the kid out."

The three men leave the room as he bends down to match Maji's eye level.

"You gave us a scare out there," he states calmly. He gestures to the window, and Maji leans forward to look out. Beyond the glass, the ocean is swelling back and forth. Gray water and rain are covering everything. Maji is happy to know that it wasn't the nasty bump on his head that kept his balance bobbing back and forth.

Relief washes over him. They haven't taken him back yet. *There's still a chance.*

The man tips his head to the side as if he can read Maji's mind. Keeping his distance, the man puts his hands in his pocket and leans against the wall.

Maji takes note of the tattoos on this man's black skin. They run around his knuckles and wrist and snake up his neck in thick bars. While he can't make sense of them, it reminds him of the print on a dangerous animal. Maji has always listened to his intuition and his senses—it's saved him on more than one occasion. So when he feels a dark fog around the man's eyes and face as if shrouded in a veil, Maji pays attention. It's not always that he can read a stranger like how he can read his mom. This tells Maji that, even with his laid-back demeanor, he should trust this man less than all the others. He has secrets.

Maji hears Mr. D's voice in his head as if on cue. *How do you navigate someone when you don't know what they want? How do you make sure you keep the power and protect yourself?*

"They call me Queen," the man states, tapping his chest. When Maji doesn't respond, he adds, "It's cuz I'm from Queens, if you're wondering."

Maji makes sure to give him nothing. Not a word. Not an expression.

"What about you? You gotta name?" Queen laughs to himself. "C'mon. I was the one who jumped in to get you. You know that? Can't do me a solid and give me anything? Do you usually go swimming in the ocean during a storm?"

"Do you usually kidnap boys?" Maji snaps back. "What are you, pedophiles?"

Maji knows how to play this game. He wants to see if he can make this guy angry. Typically, angry people make mistakes.

Queen nods in approval. "Good one, but nah. More of a cannibal myself." Queen shakes his hand out and checks his nails.

"A ... cannibal?"

Maji tries to judge the comment on Queen's face, but he sees nothing. Then, finally, fear starts crawling up his spine as Queen opens his mouth to laugh.

Maji scowls. *Did this guy flip this back on me?*

Queen waves him off. There's a gold ring on his left hand. "My bad, man. I couldn't help myself. Alright. At least give me where you from?"

"The Bronx," Maji replies.

Queen claps his hands. "Look at that. Queens. Bronx. See? That wasn't too hard."

Maji immediately regrets talking to him.

"You're kinda far from the Bronx, aren't you?"

"You're kinda far from Queens."

Queen chuckles and Maji finds it the most infuriating thing. It feels like he's talking to a damn wall. Seeing that he's struggling to sit straight on the cot, Queen adds, "That leg of yours got messed up out there. It was pretty bad, but we dressed it. Collins is our first aid guy, so you'll live, but he says you'll need stitches. Nothing we can do here, so just chill for a bit and I'll go get you something to eat."

Maji scowls at him as he walks to the door and goes through. He immediately gets up but has to dive back into bed as Queen walks back in.

"Dry pants are underneath the cot. Help yourself." Then he vanishes again.

Maji gets dressed and checks for another exit. It seems like he's at the bottom of the boat, and there is only one other room outside the door. Nothing else. No way out but through.

He nudges the door open. The next room is slightly higher and brighter. Maji spots a radio, some other equipment he can't place, and a steering wheel facing large windows. Beyond this, he can barely make out three silhouettes. Wearing ponchos, it's obvious the men have gone outside to talk about him. Maji strains his ears to listen.

A fourth man joins; more than likely, it's Queen.

"What's he say?" a man asks.

"He's from the city."

"You're kidding me?" another voice asks. The accent is the red-headed guy.

The men have to talk loud to get their voices over the water. Still, some waves drown out a few of their sentences.

"I can't explain it, but that's what he says. And yeah, I believe him. How else would a kid like him get out here?"

"No way? Did you see that raft?"

"He's probably a runaway."

"Runways go to New Jersey, Queen. This kid went out to the ocean. Is he mentally there?"

Maji can't hear if Queen responds.

"I'll go call it in. He's just lucky we came back this way. What kind of goddamn parents . . . ." This man sounds angrier than the rest as he leaves the others.

Just hearing this come out of the man's mouth makes Maji want to lunge at him, but he keeps himself together and pulls back into the room.

As he sits back down on the cot, Maji knows that he can't go back home. This is his only chance. He would be on lockdown for the rest of his life if his mom got her hands on him. Or worse? What if there's some law against what he's done? What if he ends up in Rikers?

Maji decides that he will wait for an opening and play their game—be friendly and respectful but keep his distance. *Just be patient.*

A few minutes later, Queen shows up with a small bowl of food and Maji's black duffle bag slung around his shoulder. He drops it in front of him and hands him the bowl. It's cooked chicken and probably potatoes. Maji goes into his bag instead of grabbing the bowl. Most of his chips and pastries are soaked or missing. He grabs a soggy bear claw, tears the wrapper open with his teeth, and stuffs it into his mouth.

"That'll work, too," Queen chuckles as he takes the bowl back. His voice sounds deep and with the soft rattle of a smoker. Then, he begins eating the bowl of mush himself.

Still rummaging through the bag, Maji finds no sign of the clear bags with his cell phone and book. When Maji looks up, Queen pulls the phone from his back pocket and starts going through it.

A rage fills Maji's chest. "Give me that."

"You got one hell of a playlist going on here. Tyler the Creator. Kudi. Some Common? Whatchu know about Common?"

Maji stands up and holds out his hand. The other is balled up into a fist by his waist. "I know that you better give me my phone back."

Queen holds the phone for a few seconds and flips it in his palm.

He then hands it over.

Maji snatches it to make his point, but instead of getting angry, Queen points at him. "I'm actually surprised that I didn't see one of the lil's on there."

Maji scowls. "What's a lil?"

"You know. The lil's. Lil Plop. Lil Poop. One of those rappers."

Maji stares at him. "You think there's a rapper out there named Lil Poop?"

A curly smirk appears on Queen's face, almost making Maji smile. However, he recovers and hangs on to his scowl instead.

"I don't listen to anyone like that."

"Ah well. There's something I have to ask."

"Ask whatever you want. I ain't telling you my name."

"Cool, but not the question. Check this out." Queen goes over to the metal desk and opens the laptop. He connects a speaker to the side and begins to play a song. The beat drops and Maji listens as Queen bobs his head.

"Know who this is?"

Maji thinks for a second. *Is this a trick?* "Kendrick Lamar."

Queen rocks his hand back and forth. "Nah. Sounds like him. I like Kenny, but this ain't him."

Maji listens closer.

Queen sucks his teeth. "You like J. Cole and you don't know about JID?"

After a brief listen, Queen plays it back from the beginning. He says he likes the first verse the most.

Maji flashes a fake smile and agrees that it's pretty sick. When he offers to play another, Maji tells him okay in the softest voice he can manage. His body is loose. His shoulders slump. Maji sits on the ground and crosses his legs to listen. He hopes it makes him look younger and weaker.

In reality, he is just waiting, biding his time. The moment Queen so much as blinks too long, he's going to make his move.

But he also knows that it's not going to be easy. This guy—who looks like an idiot singing with his eyes closed and snapping his long fingers to the beat—is also keeping an eye on him.

This man was the only thing keeping him from making it back to the sea.

Chapter 15 ⤳

"HEY, Bronx. Come on out and get some fresh air?"

Following Queen onto the deck, Maji can now see the entirety of the ship that saved him. The broadside is painted blue and red, with the main sections like thick, white boards. The boat has two large spotlights in the front (which Maji had previously mistaken for glowing eyes) and wide nets to fish materials out of the water.

The waves around them are breaking high, spilling water over the stubby nose of the ship.

"This is the *Americana*," Queen explains. "We typically patrol the rivers surrounding New York. This is a conservation boat, which means that our job is to make sure companies on the coastlines don't dump waste into the water. More of a problem in the 70's and 80's. Killed a lot of fish."

A memory flickers into Maji's mind. He remembers his mom writing letters and mailing them. To congressmen. To local representatives. The water in the park next to the Bronx Zoo was polluted and she wanted to fight against losing. It was the only place Maji loved to play as a kid, and she wanted to protect that. That's when his mom was still passionate about the world. Before the world had sucked away her color and music.

Maji fights back this memory as soon as he feels his lip begin to shake.

As Queen walks him to the back of the boat where everyone is working, Maji spots a plume of black smoke pouring out of one side. The men climb around the outside of the ship, hammering and sealing holes with large wooden planks. From the looks of it, the ship had taken a beating during the storm and the crew was busy trying to get it running again.

"A few days ago, someone spotted something floating down the Hudson at night. Picked it up on a camera. We usually don't come all the way out here, more accustomed to the river, like I said. But we did so just to double-check that someone didn't dump junk out here that would make things worse. Then that storm blew in, from out of nowhere really, and we had to stay put for a while. When we doubled back, that's when we saw you floating out there on your own."

Maji's focus drifts from the words coming out of Queen's mouth to the world around him. The *Americana* is a long boat painted in two tones: blue along the bottom, and white for the main cabin. Orange life preservers dangle off of the metal walkways. The boat is very narrow towards its end, but the main deck is raised like a stage. This is where most of the crew—six men in total—congregate when they want to talk or enjoy a hot cup of coffee.

Maji tries his best to search for his raft or bag, but after a full tour of the ship, there's no sign of either. Instead, he spots a tiny ship kept in a metal rack in the back of the boat—a tiny, wooden jalopy, barely able to fit a single person, with a dirty, white motor attached. He watches as the men use a thick rope to lower the boat into the water. When he can, Maji bends his entire attention to this as if he's trying to read its movements. He watches as it skims across the water. He notes how the engine shuts off every few minutes and how the guy in the boat, a man he has yet to meet, has to pull the cord and pray that it restarts.

The *Americana* lets out a thick belch as its engine tries to come to life, but all it does is sputter and then fall silent.

"Something on your mind there, Bronx?"

Sensing Queen examining him, Maji picks his words carefully. "How far are we from New York?"

"I'd say fifty miles from Long Island, give or take." The man gives him a side-eye. "Planning to swim back?"

"Are you planning on taking me back?"

"We are. I'm just wondering what we're taking you back to." Maji feels the man's eyes watching him closely. "You know the other guys are wondering about what brought you out here. They think that you might've fallen off another ship. A cruise ship? Something else? They don't believe you sailed out here by yourself."

Nice try, Maji thinks.

He shrugs and responds, "And what do you think?"

"Me?" Queen's eyes twinkle, and he sits on the floor. "I think there's more to you than what folks see there, Bronx. If you did sail out here, then aight. You did. That's all you have to say."

"Well I did," Maji responds, and he immediately hates himself. Queen had found ways to slip in between what Maji is and isn't telling him like it was his damn superpower.

Maji both hates *and* respects the guy.

"You got kids?"

Shocked to be on the receiving end of a question for once, Queen smirks. "I do. A boy. Younger than you. Same type of energy, though."

Maji and Queen stare as the smaller boat makes a full circle and pauses to restart.

ᔐ ᔐ ᔐ

Night comes pretty quickly out on the ocean. By the time someone tells Queen that dinner is ready, the repairs to the *Americana* are almost done. The waves are swelling around the ship as if rain is possible at any moment.

"I brought a book with me," Maji tells Queen while looking out into the splashing water. He keeps his eyes on the horizon and tries to keep his voice as soft as possible. "It was in my duffle bag, but it isn't there now. Probably still on the raft. I want to look for it."

He wonders if the man can see through this.

Queen shakes his head. "That thing? It might have gotten you this far, Bronx, but it ain't going to take you any further. The storm shredded it up. You're lucky to be alive." When Maji doesn't respond, he adds, "Follow me."

A minute later, they are back inside the large room, and Queen pulls the familiar book from one of the top shelves. He flicks through the pages. "The bad news is that it got soaked. I was just drying them out. Did the best I could, but it should be alright." He tosses it into Maji's arms.

Opening the leather cover, Maji passes his hand over the wrinkled splotches of water damage all along the bottom and right side. Fortunately, only the edges of the paragraphs are smudged and unreadable. He slowly closes the book.

Maji tries to compose himself. The shock of possibly losing the book makes him almost break down. He bites on the inside of his cheek to keep himself together.

The tallest man of the *Americana's* crew, a guy they call Norm, lowers his head into the room. He looks at Maji and then calls Queen over.

When the two men leave, Maji wastes no time. He's been waiting for this moment for almost the entire day. He's already scoped out the whole room and knows where he wants to search.

The desk, the filing cabinet, the high shelf.

Even though his leg is in horrible shape, Maji moves with so much deliberation that he doesn't make a single sound.

Opening small drawers. Checking corners.

He pockets everything he finds that can be useful. Scissors from the first aid kit. A pencil. An extra bandage. All the while, his ears are listening over the thump-thump of his heart. Maji has already timed all of this in his mind.

First, the door coming from the deck of the ship is rusty. The metal wails when pulled open.

An extra steep drop into the next room leads to a crunching floorboard.

Listen to that. That'll give you a few seconds.

Only a little time passes when the door creaks.

Maji keeps on his mission.

One last place.

The floorboard screams.

Maji pulls the nearest crate forward, and lying among a stack of garbage bags is a clear case that he pops open. Even though it's orange and made of plastic, the flare gun at least looks like a weapon.

The *Americana's* engine roars to life and Maji can sense

the boat lurch forward under his feet. Just outside the door, he hears Queen's voice.

"*I'll handle it. How long until we get to shore?*"

"*About an hour,*" a voice calls back.

Maji tucks the gun into the back of his pants and waits.

Queen takes one step into the room but, as if sensing something wrong, he freezes. Maji watches his eyes search around.

"I'm not going back."

"Aight, just chill."

"Don't tell me to chill."

"Okay. Relax."

"No."

Queen's movements become slow and rigid. He steps one foot over the other as if he knows what Maji is hiding.

"Tell me why you're carrying that old book around?"

"You wouldn't understand."

"The story of that whale or your story?"

"Both."

Queen is still moving towards him.

"I can only imagine what happened to you back in the city that made you go out there. I can only imagine. But you came out here with a cellphone, some food, and a book. I heard of kids running away. Hell, I was one of them back in the day. But out in the ocean? What were you looking for out here? You could've died out here."

"You don't know that."

"What about your mom? You're dad? You want them to worry?"

Hearing about his mom sets fire to Maji's skin. He fumbles with the orange gun but points it right at Queen. The man puts his hands up.

"Just calm down."

"Stop telling me to calm down."

Someone tries to push into the room to find out what's happening, but Queen stiff-arms him back. When he turns around, Maji senses a wildness in the man's eyes. Like having a weapon pointed at him flips a switch inside of him. The nice guy from Queens vanishes. In Maji's eyes, dark red vapor pours out of the man's nostrils as points.

It's the posture of old folks from the streets, a practice he seems at ease with. Even the way he speaks changes. It's like the hood is bubbling out of him. Maji can tell that even though the gun is pointed right at his chest, he isn't backing down.

"Boy, you can't be that dumb. I know you ain't that dumb. I don't care if your momma or your daddy or your auntie, or whoever, ain't shit to you. You don't put yourself in danger for no one." Queen points out of the window and yells, "What's out here for you, king? I'll tell you. Death. Nothing but an ocean that wouldn't think twice about killing a black boy. And you know what the world would care? Nothing. The world won't care a damn thing."

"What's out there is for me to find," Maji yells back. He slaps one hand over the next to keep it from shaking. "*You* don't know nothing. Not you, not anyone else. I'm going to find it. And when I do, you'll see. You'll see how right I was and everyone is going to have to listen. Everyone is going to stop what they're doing. It's all going to end. It's out there waiting for me."

Queen's eyes settle. Maji watches as the rage seems to lift from his body as purple vapor. He now looks scared and worried. His shoulders slump forward.

"Bronx, I—"

"That's not my name!"

"Okay." Queen raises his hands again. Maji can tell that he's worried about the trigger finger. "So what *is* your name?"

Maji's hands are shaking so hard that the gun's plastic rattles. He shouts into his head to *stop shaking, stop shaking,* but his muscles aren't listening.

"My name is M-M-Maji."

"Alright, Maji."

There is shouting coming from outside. It seems like someone is asking Queen to see something important.

Instead, he points back out the window. "Maji. We're headed back, okay? We gotta take you back. There's nothing that can stop that. But look at me, man. I'm the guy who jumped in for you. Me, Maji. I'm telling you, real talk, you would have died out there. You have to know that.

That book you're holding ... that's just a story. If that's what's getting you to be out here—"

The shouting from outside is getting louder. For some reason, waves make the boat rock from one side to the next. Binders and boxes fall off of the shelves and clatter to the ground. The laptop falls from the table and shatters as Maji tries to keep his footing.

"Here's some *real talk* for you," Maji says, still shaking but smiling now. "You don't know anything. You didn't see it as I did. It made the storm. It turned the water dark right in front of me. There is a miracle out here. If you don't realize that, *you'll* be the one to die. *You'll* end up dead. Just let me go and I'll show you."

Massive waves slam into the boat's side and the *Americana's* wood creaks. The men outside are shouting, now more frantically. The sound of water is so loud that Maji can't understand what they're saying. The rush of air and the booming sound echo like a massive waterfall.

Maji loses his footing and stumbles. Queen lunges at him and tries to pull the weapon out of his hands. Maji closes his eyes and starts to squeeze the trigger.

Something slams into the side of the *Americana* like a wrecking ball, sending Maji flying to the opposite side of the room. As the boat goes onto its side, Maji finds himself sliding down the wall and onto the ceiling. Shaking off the shock, he manages to dodge a desk before the metal slab crushes him flat. Queen is nowhere to be seen and doesn't respond when Maji calls his name.

As the boat falls back onto the water, the room dumps Maji right onto the floor. And in the silence after the chaos, he hears the rush of the ocean pouring in.

Chapter 16 ⌐

WHEN the sun comes up, the damage to the
Americana is out of a nightmare. Maji stands with
Queen and his crewmates on the broken deck, silently
viewing the destruction.

The back end of the ship is caved in. The right side is
torn open as if a bomb has gone off in the walls. To Maji,
the fact that the boat is still floating is a miracle.

The crew spends most of the day clearing the water out
of the lowest level, which was the only reason they weren't
in the ocean. Overhearing the conversation between the
crew, Maji finds out that while the engine is still in one
piece, the ways to steer the boat have been damaged beyond

repair. "We're going to have to float for now until someone comes to pick us up," a man named Buck grumbles. Maji watches as Queen and the other crewmates, with their tired faces and beaten bodies, slump over like this is the worst news possible.

Maji sits around as the crew works to fix the radio. The anticipation puts knots in his stomach. Last night's disaster might have bought him a few hours, but it was just a matter of time before they would contact someone. *And then this will all be over.*

The sea is calm and blue. The sight of a wrecked boat on its surface seems to clash in Maji's mind.

Maji can't help but feel that the other crew members hate him. This had all been routine before he had gotten on board. Now the boat was wrecked and they were just drifting aimlessly. While none of the men go out of their way to show their disgust, Maji can't help but feel like he's to blame.

Maji sits outside, wraps himself in a blanket, and watches the men try to repair the ship. He pays particular attention to Bishop, the older man in the rickety motorboat, as he skims across the water's surface.

A hand slams down on his shoulder.

"Keep your eyes in your head, king," Queen jokes. "I can hear those gears of yours turning in your head. But best believe that you would be better off trying to paddle out in a toilet than using that thing. That's Bishop's pail. She turns like a garbage truck and is as temperamental as his ex-wife."

He hands Maji a small plastic bowl with two apples rolling inside. As he takes one, Queen slides down beside him and takes the other. Maji looks at the man's bandaged arm and winces. The link between them is still so strong that the pain seems to leap into Maji's own forearm and joint as if it's about to break.

While they sit there watching the sea, Maji wonders why the man hasn't brought up what happened between them. Part of him is relieved that it hasn't come up. But the guilt climbs into his throat and makes it hard to breathe.

Maji opens his mouth to apologize, but Queen cuts him off.

"I'm glad you didn't get hurt." His eyes are still watching the ocean.

Maji mouths a few things. "I'm alright. You?"

"Maybe dislocated." Queen flexes his arm. "It's also coming off an old ball injury, so this bump didn't do it any favors."

"You play ball?"

Queen side-eyes him. "Boy, I *can* play ball. Don't look at me like that. I may be old, but I can give you the sauce. I used to play in tournaments."

"Ever played in the Cage?"

"Over on West 4th? Hell yeah. More than once. Was in a summer league, until I got hurt that is."

A dull weight of regret sets on the back of Maji's neck when he mentions that basketball court. He struggles with his next words. He knows what he has to say, but it comes out jumbled. Maji breathes and tries again. "Thanks for saving me."

Ever since they first met, Maji has been able to sense a darkness in Queen. He had originally misread this as something evil and dangerous. But now, watching as his words lift the dark cloud off of Queen's face, he realizes that the darkness is more of a burden. He wonders if it's about the son Queen mentioned. Whatever was eating away at this man, whatever secret was keeping him up at night, lifts like the break in a fever. Maji was always able to do this for his mom. This is the first time he has seen a change in a stranger.

He tells himself that this is what his mission is all about: freeing people from the weight they are carrying. Maji has seen so many men like Queen on his block. They walk around crushed under the concrete; the city forming a cage around their restless bodies. And they throw themselves against the bars.

Men, tortured by a system, now torturing themselves.

"The radio's fixed. They should be sending a boat to pick us up soon."

Queen groans and stands up. Instead of walking, he stops at a crate and digs through it. Finding Maji's book again, Queen hands it to him and says,

"You keep losing this."

As Queen leans over the rail and quietly watches the sea grow restless, Maji's heart sinks. He hates himself for what happened the night before. But, when he turns back in his memory, he realizes what the trigger was: Queen mentioning his mom.

Maji hangs onto the rail and rests his head on the wet bar. Something had called him out to sea. In his mind, this made him special. Whatever had appeared to him—just off of the coast of Coney Island, whatever had been in his dreams for weeks—had to be a sign that Maji was chosen. For the city. For his family.

With his feet dangling off the side of a ship in the middle of the ocean, Maji feels a rotten pit swell in his stomach. He misses his mom. It's more than that—he misses having a connection to her and her emotions. He's seen her fall ill several times; each brought on because of a moment of stress: when Maji had broken his arm on a playground, his first school suspension. The first time Maji had run away, his father had managed to drag him back home. As a result of the stress, his mother landed in the hospital for two weeks. Maji couldn't visit her because the hospital had very special rules.

He closes his eyes and hopes this is the last time.

It's not just his mom. He braves the water for her. For everyone.

Just one miracle. They need just one.

Maji turns the book's pages on his lap. More water spots have eaten through the pages, and the first few chapters are now impossible to read. As he pulls the pages apart, he looks up as Queen tries to leave quietly.

"What was it, Queen? What hit us last night?"

The man stops and slides his hands into his pocket. Then, without turning, he responds, "The crew says the ocean went crazy—something they had never seen before. And that's saying a lot because some of them have been sailing longer than I've been walking."

Queen takes a long breath as if the following few words out of his mouth seem impossible to him.

"They said a tail hit us," he says, "A twenty-foot tail belonging to the biggest whale they had ever seen in their lives."

Chapter 17 ᵔ

MAJI tries to ask Queen more about the whale, but he doesn't seem to want to give him answers. At first, Maji feels that Queen is trying to keep the information to himself for some reason. However, with the way Queen follows Maji's every step around the boat, it becomes obvious that he's keeping quiet as a way of making sure Maji stays put until help arrives.

"A rogue wave. That's all it was," Norm replies when Maji asks. The other men seem to agree. But not Bishop. He isn't someone Maji often saw since he worked on the small boat most of the time. But the night after the *Americana* was almost smashed to bits; he knows what he saw.

"Almost three stories. The fucker was big as hell." When Queen smacks him on the arm, he throws his hands up and grunts. "What do you want me to say? That bastard was huge."

Maji leans in. "And it was a whale?"

"Bishop's been sailing for years," Queen explains.

"Eh, eh. Not just here, either. Was a fisherman for a span before that. I lost my virginity on this water."

Queen closes his eyes.

Maji laughs. Maybe it's Bishop's accent (a gruff English tongue that usually ends with a spit or a curse). Perhaps it's how his black beard slowly turns white as it runs into his hair. Maybe it's the way his eyes seem extra wide and wild. Whatever it is, he looks like he's the only other person on this ship, outside of Queen, that isn't being fake. If he said he saw a whale, then it was a whale.

"Are they usually that big?" Maji asks

"Some. I heard some going up to 90 feet. Imagine that? Almost half the size of a football field. Whatever it was last night, was bigger than that. I'm telling you, we're lucky to even be breathing right now."

Queen crosses his arms. "What does that mean, B? You saying that it meant not to kill us?"

"I'm saying that that tail was bigger than a bus—at least thirty-five, forty feet from tip to tip. If that thing wanted us dead, we would be. I'll take the love tap we got any day." As he says this, Bishop thrusts his finger at the destroyed back end of the *Americana*.

"We got company," someone at the back of the ship yells.

Maji looks up at Queen, and they both walk outside to where the crew is gathering.

In the distance, Maji can see the last of the dying light slowly folding into darkness. In front of this backdrop, he sees a boat sailing toward them. Maji senses something wrong and looks over at Queen's face.

"Hey, Con. Didn't you say they would be here in a few hours? It hasn't even been thirty minutes." Queens leans forward. "Who are these clowns?"

Dread climbing into his skin, Maji tries looking out. The bad lightning and his horrible vision make it difficult to see, but his eyes adjust just slightly enough to make it out. The boat is smaller than the *Americana* and it seems to be racing toward them. On the white part of the cabin, blue letters are printed on the side.

NYPD.

A terror reaches right into Maji's guts and crushes them. *No. It can't be.*

His first instinct is to run, but Queen grabs his arm before he moves an inch.

His eyes are serious; focused. "They haven't seen you yet. Get downstairs."

Maji staggers to his feet. "I—"

"Move your ass. Get downstairs. Find someplace to hide."

Con asks, "What are you doing, Queen?"

Ignoring his crewmate, Queen shoves the book into his arms and pushes Maji away.

Maji runs down to the lower level and looks for a place to hide. The entire room is destroyed and sogged in knee-deep ocean water, so finding a hiding place initially seems impossible. He pushes over an empty metal locker and sets it upright. It smells horrible inside, but he slams the door behind him.

The broken gap in the wall allows Maji to see the ocean. The sound of the ship motor getting closer seems to shake him into pieces.

Maji hears a voice call over to the other boat. It's Queen.

"Good evening, officers. Kinda far for a 9-1-1 call."

A voice shouts through a bullhorn on the other ship. *"Throw over a line. Are your engines off?"*

This doesn't sound like someone is coming to help. These are orders.

"Sorry but uh, we lost our line when we got hit."

"Cut your engines off. Now."

"Our engines are off, man. Chill!

Maji can see the edge of the other boat creep closer. The hole only allows him to see the edge of the ship itself. He makes out the shape of two men on the front of the boat.

"We are coming aboard. Back up."

A loud sound echoes through the boat as the two collide, followed by a loud splash behind the boat.

"What's that?" a stranger's voice asks.

Maji sees flashlight beams checking the surface of the water.

"That's the sound of you knocking my pail boat into the water, you ass."

Leave it to Bishop to speak his mind, Maji thinks.

There are several footsteps walking along the boat now. A set goes to the back of the ship, probably to inspect the damage. A few muffled voices are talking. The only one Maji hears is Queen.

"It's just us, man."

An angry voice responds though it's too far to make out.

"The kid? We had him for a bit, but he got on his raft and left when we were trying to fix it up. Ain't that right guys?"

Maji can't hear if anyone else agrees. A dull pain is forming in his neck.

Is Queen lying for me?

There is shouting between Queen and someone else, the second figure who had come over on that NYPD boat. A loud shuffle of feet. Someone stomps into the lower level, splashing as he arrives, and Maji throws himself back to the rear of the locker just as they enter the room.

Whoever is there is turning things over. Searching. He's looking for him.

Maji hears Queen arrive and, as if he knows where Maji is hiding, stands between this police officer and the locker. Maji peeks through the slit in the door, but he doesn't recognize the officer standing there.

"I told you that he isn't here. He got away."

The officer stares directly at Queen and probes around with his flashlight. Compared to Queen, the cop is much taller and more imposing than his smaller frame. His shoulders are broad, and the belt around his waist holding his taser and gun rattles. Just as he's about to say something, the second man runs into the room and pushes Queen to the side.

When Maji realizes this is his father, the air leaves his lungs.

Maji's father draws a cell phone from his pocket and shoves the screen in Queen's face. "Is this the kid that was here?"

To Maji, his voice sounds like the rumble of thunder, or is this happening outside as well?

Queen takes the phone and walks away from the locker. Maji can see his face now, illuminated by the screen.

"Where did you get this picture?"

"Answer the question."

"Yeah. I think but—"

"You think or you know?"

"Look, man. He wasn't here for long. He got hurt on the water. We gave him first aid and in the confusion last night, he got away. We would've gone after him—"

"Save it." Maji's dad snatches the phone away.

It's then that Maji realizes that the other police officer doesn't have the uniform of a typical cop. The shirt has padding on the sides and white bars on the sleeve. The patch on his chest reads "NYPD POLICE Harbor Unit."

"You know if you're keeping information during a police investigation, you'll be in violation of your parole."

Maji watches as anger grows on Queen's face. The dark cloud Maji thought he had lifted from this man's soul returns and begins to swell. "What the fuck do you know about my parole?"

"Again. Is that kid in the picture here or not?"

Maji's stomach drops. Queen looks both terrified and enraged. Like he's about to snap at any moment.

Maji's dad shoves the screen in his face again. "His name's Imajin, goes by Maji. He's sixteen. His mother is worried. He's probably confused, possibly looking to harm himself."

Queen stares at him, not the phone. "It takes a whole police boat to come pick up one boy? That's why you have to look me up, drag up my past? Because a kid ran away?"

Maji's father lowers his hand slowly.

Maji feels the anxiety flooding his small compartment. The air of violence is climbing into his mouth and nose. He feels strangled by the pressure in the room. He wants to call out, but his jaw doesn't move. Maji is frozen in fear.

"Kind of a long way for a single cop to come for a kid," Queen states, crossing his arms.

Maji's dad continues looking around the room as he replies, "Say what you mean or shut your mouth."

Queen moves out of Maji's view. Maji's father is reaching out to check Maji's locker when he says, with a growl,
"*You're* the one who came *here* —throwing your weight
around. Throwing my past in my face. So who are you
really?"

Maji can see his father's face as Queen's words seem
to tear into him. He whips around, and Maji watches his
father draw his gun.

Queen holds his hands up.

Maji's limbs begin to shake. This is the same as before,
only he was the one pointing the gun. Only now, Maji feels
like a bystander; a spirit. He has flashes of memories to
the videos, the body cams, the social media posts. And the
names spill out of Maji like a stream of pain.

Daunte Wright Andre Hill Stephon Clark Botham Jean

So many names. So many.

And here, right in front of him, Maji is witnessing the
hole open again. The hole that he has seen swallow up so
many people.

"You want to know who I am?" his father growls. "I'm
someone that isn't going to lose sleep if I smoke you right
here. I want to know how a boy goes from his bed in the
Bronx to a boat in the middle of the Atlantic. So yeah, I
got someone to run your jacket, to run everyone's profile on
this boat. And the only person in my face when I get here
is the one with the largest rap sheet. A violent drugee—"

"That's my past, man!"

"Not if I say so."

"Put the gun down, Eli." The other cop's voice is stern.

Both Queen and Maji's father stare at each other.

Maji feels like he's going to blackout. His body feels so tense that he's turning to stone. His tongue is raw, a rash on the inside of his mouth. There is a siren shrieking between his ears. It's getting louder and louder. Maji feels like clawing at his face.

The officer places his hand slowly over the gun and takes it out of Eli's hand.

Queen, not even missing a beat, says, "You know I came out to the water to avoid being shot."

"Why did you kidnap Maji and what did you do with him?"

Maji tries to scream, but no sound comes out. Fighting against the pain he's feeling, his legs come to life and he kicks the inside of the locker. The sound should have given him away, but at precisely the same time, someone shouts from the back of the ship.

"You have to get up here quick!"

Eli and the officer seem so possessed by this that they ignore the sound and race upstairs.

Queen lowers his shaking hands and looks around the room before chasing after them.

Maji throws himself against the door, but it doesn't move. Instead, it seems pinned behind an outstretched plank of wood. Refusing to let go of the book in his arms, he kicks the door twice. But the force only causes the locker to fall backward where it hits the floor, rolls and slips out of the broken part of the wall.

Feeling the wound on his leg stretch and reopen, Maji tumbles in this metal prison before he hears a splash, and seawater starts to flood through the gaps in the door.

Panicking, he tries to push it open, but the door doesn't budge.

The water is up to his neck now.

Maji continues to kick and tread water, but it saps his strength. The only pocket of air is at the top of the locker, and Maji keeps his chin up while he tries to catch a breath. Holding one in his lungs, he drops down and throws his whole body against the door.

The metal peels open into the darkness of the deep.

Unable to kick with his injured leg and one arm still gripping the book, Maji struggles to get on top of the water.

At first, he tries to grasp the edge of the locker, but it quickly fills with water and sinks. Maji is coughing and spitting out water. He tries to keep quiet, but it's impossible when you can't breathe. No one seems to notice. No one comes running or shouts his name.

But I'm going to drown.

He considers letting go of the book and calling out . . .

Something drifts close to his head, and Maji panics only to find that it's the back of Bishop's drifting boat.

Tossing the book in, Maji uses all his strength to drag himself into the wooden boat. When he does, he has to lay there as spots float around his eyes and his lungs burn. His leg pain wails. He turns to his side to throw up. What comes out is saltwater and hot bile.

A flashlight beam crosses over the top of his boat, and Maji lays still as the beam skims silently past his head.

He hears a voice yelling, "Tell me now. What is this?"

Maji peeks over the edge only to see his father holding his black duffle bag. The spotlight lights up his face. It's so cold that smoke pours out of his nostrils. He slams the items on the ground and runs into the boat calling out Maji's name. Everyone chases after him.

He could turn himself in. He could go back with his father. But Maji remembers that there's nothing to go back to. *If I go back now, my school life will end. My family will end. And without this, what will happen to me?*

Suddenly a streak of lightning cuts across the black night sky. It's nothing like he has ever seen before. The jagged shard of bluish light travels much longer and slower than any typical lightning crack, almost like massive cracks have formed in the night sky. Maji follows it away from the scene on the deck to where it lands several miles behind him.

As it dies and the darkness returns, Maji sees the silhouette of something in the distance. It looks big enough to be land, but Maji senses it is moving.

A roll of thunder shakes the ocean and the sky. The waves begin to froth and rise.

Maji dangles an arm over the edge of the tiny boat and tries to gain momentum by stroking the water with his hands. Maji tries his best not to splash water, but he finds himself going nowhere with his lack of strength and the power in the waves.

On a clear night like this, Maji will need the tiny boat's engines to escape. Plus, the NYPD boat could catch up to him in no time.

Another wicked bolt of lightning leaves its imprint on the black canvas. And just like before, it slowly curls around the sky and strikes the same dark silhouette in the distance.

Whatever is out there is calling to him.

Maji gets an idea. Rolling to his side, he grips the chord to start the engine like he saw Bishop do. He looks at the sky. He has to time this right.

Please start on the first try, he thinks. *Please, please.*

The thunder comes louder and longer than before. It sounds like a beast roaring. The ocean receives it like an order, and the waves rise.

With a long tug of his arm, Maji pulls the cord to match the booming sound in the air. The engine clicks and turns on. Maji's boat goes forward five feet and stops as the engine knocks out again.

No, no, no!

Someone comes out of the lower deck and beams the flashlight into the water. Maji has to drop down again.

Please, please, please.

When the next bolt of lightning comes, it's brighter, sharper, and sports several branches of light that seem to fly everywhere like fireworks.

While still on his stomach, Maji grabs the chord and closes his eyes.

The thunder that follows is more of an explosion. It bubbles the water and scares Maji into pulling the cord.

The engine kicks on.

The boat pushes itself through the heavy waves as the thunder continues to bounce across the edges of the earth. Maji lies out of breath as he's taken far away from the *Americana*. The angry voices grow quiet over the rattle of the pail's engine.

Maji grips the book close to his chest.

I will make it. I will. I must.

Chapter 18 ⌐

MAJI carefully unwraps the bandage on his leg and instantly starts gagging. The smell hits him first; it reaches into his nostrils and makes him kick his head back. It smells like rotten garbage. The blood on the gauze is not red; it's yellow-brown. The skin around the hole in his leg is wrinkled and graying. The meat beneath is slimy.

Maji cups his hand and scoops up seawater. Before he splashes it on his leg, he takes a few breaths. He screams as a few drops spill into the wound, so he dumps the entire thing. It feels like he's pouring acid on his skin.

Vowing *never* to do that again, he rewraps the leg. He doesn't have a clean dressing, so he uses the parts of the old one that is clear of blood. He then collapses, out of breath and exhausted.

He props up his cell phone against the wedge of the boat and removes the battery. The phone was in his pocket when he was dunked into the ocean the previous night, so he's been trying his best to air it out.

Snapping the battery back into place, he hits the power button and stares up at the screen. It lights up, but there is a black smudge beneath the cracked face like a birthmark—only the edges of the screen work when he presses his finger to scroll.

At least it turns on.

The speakers sound muffled, so Maji puts it up against his ear. He must have hit his tracklist because it's playing. From how the beat pops and the vocals, Maji knows it's the song "Moonlight."

He closes his eyes and listens for a while before getting up.

The engine died a long time ago. It managed to run almost all night before sputtering out, and, in that time, Maji had fallen asleep. Maybe it was the boat rocking or the fact that he was coming down from his adrenaline rush, but Maji had taken one long look around to see that his tiny boat was not being followed and then fell asleep, wet clothes and all.

After rewrapping his leg, Maji takes a look out on the

horizon. There is a small black huddle of shapes, but they aren't growing larger. They must have thought that the pail had been pushed off by itself in the night, giving him the window he needed to escape.

Maji was shocked that his father would come out this far to find him. People have said that Maji inherited his headstrong (and thick-headed) personality from his dad. Even if this is true, this is the same man who has spent the last year slowly disappearing from his life. How did he know Maji was on the *Americana*? No one else knew of his plan to come out to sea.

Without the motor, Maji is now just drifting. In the beginning, he had some control over his speed and direction. Now he's without a sail, without food or water, and with only a soggy book for comfort.

He remembers Queen's warning about the ocean, and it turns his stomach. Instead of giving in to this, Maji knows he only has one option now.

I have to find it. Whatever called to me last night. If I see it, this can all be over.

Since he's alone, Maji removes his pants and hangs them on the edge of the pail to dry. He keeps his shirt on—the sun is the last thing he needs directly on his skin.

He opens the book and tries to read to pass the time, but a few soggy pages tear off in his hand. Cursing to himself, he tosses the wet lump aside. Only the middle chapters have escaped the running ink that has spread to the center of the book.

Maji can't find the story in his memory, so he reads until his hunger cries out from his belly. Then, to avoid thinking about it, he forces himself to sleep.

～ ～ ～

When Maji wakes, the night's stars are out. A quick look out at the horizon reveals no approaching boats. Not even dots. He breathes a sigh of relief.

Hours pass. The hunger is now worse than before. There's nothing in the boat for supplies other than a thick rope coiled up in the back.

Maji picks it up and holds it flat in his hands. Then, shaking his head, he decides, *There's no damn way I'm eating a rope.*

The only light is the moon which forms a perfect oval in the dark water around his boat. It's impossible to tell if the listless boat has drifted in any direction. It's like Maji is floating in a blank space—alone, empty.

It's in this quiet that Maji feels homesick again. He wants to believe that his mission—the very reason he sailed out here a few days ago—is for something good to happen in his life for a change. For something good to finally happen to everyone.

With the world crumbling around him and his family falling apart in front of his eyes, Maji had gone to the sea to find something that would make life worth living. To find something that no one has ever seen. To find something so impossible that everything everyone seems to care about these days—hatred, racism, death—would come second to his miracle.

If Maji can find the white whale from the story, the world will have to throw out everything it knows about this life. Science, religion. It will prove that there's something special about the world. That miracles and beauty exist. That there's something special about life and, in turn, something special about Maji.

As he exhales and looks up at the moon, Maji hears something out in the water.

Splashing.

Something just on the edge of the darkness surfaces and then dips down.

Maji tucks his cell phone into his pocket so that he can listen. From what he can tell, it's about ten feet from his boat. He can't see what it is, but it brings him to life.

He plunges his hand into the water. He bangs on the side of the boat. Maji jumps up and down and waves his arms, even with his bad leg. He yells so much that his voice cracks in the night air.

Whatever is out in the water seems to stop and listen.

"I'm right here," he shouts. "Come on! I'm right here!"

Only silence.

Frantically, Maji leans over again and dunks his arm into the dark water.

Maji stops splashing to listen.

The night grows so silent that the waves seem to stand still.

With his hand still dipped into the ocean to his elbow and his face hovering just an inch from the water, Maji closes his eyes and prays. He waits. For a sign. For redemption.

When he reopens them, he finds himself looking down at his reflection. The moonlight has turned his small pocket of the ocean into a mirror for just a few seconds.

Maji doesn't recognize himself. His eyes may still be round like his mom's, and his head may still be long like his dad's, but the boy in the water does not seem like him. It doesn't look like a boy at all. Instead, Maji sees himself as if he's aged a hundred years. His lips are chapped and broken. His swollen eyes and cheeks make him look as if he hasn't slept in weeks.

Maji looks beyond this reflection, beyond the surface of the lapping skin of the Atlantic. A dark object is down there, first the size of a fist and then a melon.

Something is rising to meet his submerged hand.

The dark silhouette is surfacing.

Maji squints into the water as the shadows grows. Three feet across.

Four feet.

Seven feet.

At the last second, Maji jerks his arm out of the water and drops back into the boat just as the shark's head breaks the surface.

The force is too much for the little motorboat to handle. Half of the boat lifts into the air as the shark tries to tip the whole thing over. Terrified, Maji throws himself onto the floor, hoping to stay inside the tiny boat. But with the massive shark underneath it, the left side keeps rising and seems ready to tip him right into the black water.

Maji watches as the book slides to the side of the boat and lands flat on the edge where the wood meets the water. It's about to slip into the ocean, but the boat slams back down just before it does.

Maji is shaking. His body feels like it's tied in knots. There's pain shooting throughout his legs and arms, and he dares not move.

Outside, he can hear the predator making large circles around the boat.

Chapter 19

MAJI is back in the metal locker. It begins to fill with black water that looks like ink. Maji uses his arms and legs to tread, to stay above the surface, but his right leg doesn't work. When he looks down, it's missing—nothing but a stump. Around him, the metal begins to scream. And then he feels the walls crunch down over his arms and legs.

The air is gone. The light is gone.

He tries the door, and it flies open, spilling him out like hot vomit. Even with his leg missing, Maji feels he has to run. He hears a voice, one filled with anger. It's shouting his name over and over.

When he does get up to run, he's not underwater anymore. Instead, he is leaping from one rooftop to the next. He doesn't know how, but he knows someone is chasing him. This man's gun holster rattles as he jumps after Maji.

He doesn't dare to look over his shoulder. He feels that if he does, he will fall.

Suddenly, he feels the figure closing behind him.

He reaches out and grabs Maji by the collar.

"Imajin," the male voice says.

And then Maji falls.

The sidewalk is speeding towards him. There are people below, not paying attention to the boy about to splatter on the concrete. They walk and carry on with their lives.

Chapter 20 ⤳

Maji is dripping in sweat when he wakes up, and there are so many white spots in his vision that he thinks there are spotlights on him again. As they fade, he realizes that it's nighttime. Had he slept through the day, or was it the same night? Maji can't tell.

The pain in his leg is now reaching down to his ankle and climbing up onto his hip. His back is stiff, and the fever rises from his skin like a furnace. Maji gets on all fours and looks over the edge of the boat. The night sky is cloudy, and the moon is gone, but he can see for yards around the ship. There's no sign of the random pieces of the boat.

The thick waves creep across the surface of the ocean like mounds. They lap against the underside of his beaten boat. Maji watches each one, filling himself with dread every time one comes crashing against the ship. In his mind, a predator can be lurking beneath every one.

He sits quietly and doesn't move a muscle.

A question is seeded in his mind, one that he shakes off. He's afraid to give it to the universe. But after what feels like an hour, he allows it to bloom.

What if it left?

Maji has an idea to check. He will grab the nearby rope and fling it as far as possible. The splash would get the attention of whatever's out there. Then he would see. Then he would know.

To prepare, Maji rolls his shoulder over and turns to face the other end of the boat.

This tiny movement is all the shark needs.

It's almost four times the size of Maji. The top of the shark looks slick and black in the moonlight. Its underbelly is white. Maji feels like it has more teeth in its mouth than possible. But the worst part of this creature is its eyes: blacker than the night, lifeless and cold.

The creature leaps out of the water and slams into the rear of the boat. The force pushes the small vessel forward, causing Maji to faceplant into the ship's wooden floor. Maji's lips are so dry that they burst open instantly. He tastes the thickness of his blood.

When he recovers, Maji realizes that the back end is missing. The motor splashes into the black water and is dragged away by a wave. Instinctively, Maji reaches out to grab it before the engine sinks, but the shark immediately plucks the machine from the surface and disappears.

Maji drags himself as far back as he can as the back end of the boat, now just jagged splinters, begins to sink beneath the surface.

Maji's phone tumbles into the water. He watches the light from the shattered screen sink into nothingness.

He wonders if this is another nightmare—if he's going to wake up before the seawater swallows him up.

Will he wake up on a raft?

On the *Americana*?

Or will he wake up in his bed in the South Bronx?

Maji tries to keep himself awake as he crawls to the front end of the broken pail. Measuring only five feet across, barely enough for him to curl his legs to avoid touching the water, it is the only part of the boat not underwater.

Maji watches the middle of the boat sink beneath the surface.

But just as it reaches his end, it stops.

Maji waits.

Waits for the nightmare to end.

He waits for the familiar softness of his bed covers and his pillow's push against his cheek. He waits to see the single beam of sunlight that usually lands on his face and wakes him up during the mornings.

He waits and waits.

But the nightmare doesn't end.

Chapter 21 ⌐

THE last thing Maji remembers eating was back on the *Americana*. It was an apple Queen had tossed him. At first, he had thought of turning it down because Maji normally doesn't do apples, but he devoured that one, skin and all.

The last time he remembers Queen smiling is when he took the gnawed core from him.

The last thing he remembers of his mom is telling her goodbye in her bedroom.

Lying for hours in this scooped position puts cramps in Maji's back and legs. Most of his body is numb, from the tips of his fingers to his toes. He wants to move, to stretch out his limbs and grab a full breath, but what choice does he have?

Maji knows that along with the gash in his inner lip, getting saltwater into his leg wound will hurt like hell. His fever burns through his clothes, and a yellow crust has formed over the hole in his leg.

Time moves slow. The numbness has spread all over his body and it's made his movements sluggish. He tries to open his eyes, but can't be sure if he's looking up at the sky or down at the water. The waves dip and splash, but he watches them as if the world is mute.

Maji tries to move his neck, but a moan leaves his lips instead. The sound that pours out of his mouth and throat reminds him of a dying animal.

The only thing he's grateful for is that the boat, or whatever's left of it, hasn't sunk any further. Even as the large waves of the Atlantic beat against its sides. Even as Maji's weight bears down on the weakest end. Maji tries to think of a strategy to get out of this mess, but everything in his mind is fog.

When daylight arrives, the water is blue: bluer than he's ever seen. The sun is out, but all it does is cause streaks in his eyes. It's bright, but he doesn't feel the weather around him. To him, the fire burning beneath his skin is all that matters. There's no sign of the shark, but Maji can sense it stirring in the water. He knows the creature could quickly sink the boat, but it chooses not to. It doesn't make sense, but this is what he believes with his heart and soul.

I'm going to die.

Maji fights against this thought with every ounce of energy he has left; every shred of happiness he has managed to hang onto this entire time. But it has its claws in him now. He's at the mercy of the ocean now.

With the pain and discomfort, his hunger and dehydration, and the fever rising from a rotting wound—Maji's sense of time is gone. He can't remember how many days he's been out in the ocean. While he can remember that apple Queen gave him, he can't recall when it happened. How many days has it been since he escaped the *Americana*? When had the shark attacked? How long has he been floating on the edge of a sinking boat? The last day of school? The last time he rode a train?

A thought appears in his mind. It starts small but balloons over time. Finally, after a few hours of hanging listlessly on the edge of the boat, Maji stares into the water.

The sun and the ocean: these all-powerful things that Maji had taken for granted living in a small two-bedroom apartment in the Bronx. Now, rocking helplessly on its surface, Maji realizes that the sea doesn't care for him; the ocean doesn't need him. The moment it decides, the water will roll over and crush him flat—wipe Maji out instantly. There have been times in his life when Maji has felt small and insignificant. Yet nothing has ever matched the powerlessness he feels in this moment.

I can't . . . .

I can't stay another night here.

The ocean should have been something special. Something magical. Once the sun is gone, Maji knows that his life will be over. He's hung on for as long as he can. He's tried and tried, but now he knows: Queen was right. There is nothing but death waiting for him out in the sea. Not hope. Not happiness. Just more of his life back home: threats upon his life, fighting for survival; the lifeless eyes of predators on his black skin.

Maji loosens his grip and falls limp onto the floor of the boat. He doesn't have the energy to brace himself. His hearing is still gone, so his body thumping on the wet wood only sounds loud in his head.

With his body submerged down to his chin, even the cold jet of the Atlantic does nothing to calm his fever. He can't even feel the deep cut in his leg. There's something else here, digging into the side of his neck. The book! He was lying on the book this entire time.

Maji grabs it with one arm and brings it close to his chest.

His muscles ache. With every breath, pain enters his lungs in the form of a hot knife. He can barely see the sun, and this terrifies him. The night will come with pain and horrors. He has no control over this.

At least if I do it myself . . . Maji thinks but doesn't go any further. Instead, he drags himself closer to the ocean. He watches as a cloud of his blood drifts along the water and, almost instantly, a dark shape rises out of some twenty feet away.

146

Maji can't feel his legs and arms. He regrets everything: coming out to the sea, running away from home. He wants to throw himself entirely into the water—give himself to the ocean and be done with it. He was stupid. Stupid to think that he was special. Stupid to believe that there was anything powerful and beautiful in the world. In the end, he is just going to be another dead boy checked off the list.

He sees the shark's head rise from the water. Its throat is wide. The teeth lining its mouth hang like gruesome thorns.

But it gets no further.

A dull pop leaps into the air as the side of the shark's head explodes. And then its eye. Wounded, the shark dives downward, leaving a large pool of blood behind on the surface. Just as his head goes underwater, Maji reads the white letters printed on the side: NYPD.

Maji's thoughts don't feel connected to his body. As his mind slows to a crawl, the salt water rushes in through his mouth and nose. The world beneath the surface feels vast; endless. To Maji, this is where peace is. Where everything makes sense in a way that he has never known possible.

At first, it's just Maji and the sea. But then a large body jumps in beside him. Pressed against this man's chest, Maji's mind plays a memory for him to see. He is five years old. In a park, he is running, hiding, and doing his best not to get caught. Eventually, the man who has been chasing him bundles him up in his arms. Maji remembers laughing and giggling. It's maybe the happiest he's ever been.

Maybe the safest he's ever felt. The man holding him in this memory is laughing, too.

As his mind slowly drifts in and out of this dream, Maji wonders why he is seeing this now. Who is this stranger kicking against the darkness beside him? Who is trying to drag him from the depths?

The questions echo in his mind as his body is dragged up to the surface.

And for the first time in what feels like an eternity, Maji takes a deep breath.

Part 3 ～～～
The Miracle

Chapter 22 ⌐

WHEN Maji opens his eyes, he finds himself staring up—not at a blue sky—but at a long, flat, brown ceiling. The soft splashing of falling waves seems so distant.

He passes his hand across his face only to find his movement sluggish; certain body parts come alive one aching extremity at a time. His throat and mouth are sore, so his voice rasps out like a dry heave.

Sitting up slightly, he sees that he's on a boat much smaller than the *Americana*. A single-pole cuts down the center of the space, and just beyond it sits two chairs in front of several control panels. In the darkness, it looks like one of the panels is covered in thick blankets. Radios and black-wired microphones dangle off several ceiling sections above these boards. Orange and red lights give the darkened cabin a soft glow like a nativity scene.

Maji feels the calluses on his fingertips and palms; the pain sparks the memory of holding onto the side of his broken boat for dear life. The wood had sliced into his fingernails. The cold water numbed his skin.

Maji's memory is hazy. He can't remember how he got into this small space. And so he goes back . . .

The *Americana* . . .

Queen . . .

The broken boat . . .

The shark . . .

Maji takes the blanket off and bundles himself up before trying to stand. The wound on his thigh is redressed with a white bandage and gauze, but the pain makes his entire leg feel rotted and hollow. He takes a step and stumbles, knocking the cot over.

The large body he had mistaken for a thick blanket flicks the lights on inside the cabin and stands to his feet. And for the first time in what seems like a lifetime, Maji finds himself face-to-face with his father.

His father is three times as big as Maji, with broad shoulders, and his hair is thinning and graying simultaneously. He has broad shoulders and sharp brown eyes—features that have led him through several athletic conquests over the years. He graduated top in his class as an NYPD recruit and has never looked back. Yet, in this lighting, he seems aged. There's even a little white patch growing around his beard.

As soon as they lock eyes, Maji thinks his father is about to rush towards him. Instead, Maji watches him purse his lips together as if they are the last line of defense against what he wants to say. He swallows these words and nods instead.

"You're awake."

His first instinct is to rush over and give his father the hug to end all hugs. But when his father retakes his seat without so much as a comment, this feeling fades away.

The lines on this man's face sharpen and flex in the dim light. Maji recognizes this as the look his father usually takes before he loses his cool.

Many years ago, when they lived by Fordham Road in a six-floor walk-up that Maji wasn't particularly fond of, Maji used to play soccer on the roof. He would slip up through the fire escape and onto the black tar to kick a ball against the fire exit door. One day Maji let his leg fly, causing the ball to sail down to the street below, tearing off one of the side mirrors of a parked car that just so happened to belong to their neighbor.

Maji's dad had the same face then that he has now.

"Can't get anyone on the radio." He slides the microphone back onto the silver hook. "Figured to make a bee-line back to the *Americana* before daylight, but it got dark too fast and I had to cut the engine off. Police radio's have a range, so I can't even call the harbor

sergeant who sailed out with me. Not that he'd appreci-
ate me stealing his boat and leaving him behind when I
chased after you."

Maji looks outside. It's so dark that there might as well
be a black sheet covering the window. "Do you even know
what you're doing?"

"Do you?"

It's the type of comment that either starts an argument
or finishes one. Maji keeps his mouth shut as his dad takes
out his cell phone and flips it open. Maji remembers when
he would crack a joke about how dated his dad's phone
was. He tries to remember how old he was when this was
part of their routine, and he's shocked to realize that it was
just last summer.

"Still no bars," his father huffs and shuts the phone.
Then, almost as if he can read the question right out of
Maji's eyes, he adds, "If you have to know, I stole this boat.
They told me not to go after you, Maji. And if I listened
to them—if I just sat my hands and waited . . . . Just be
grateful that I found you when I did."

While he isn't going to admit it, Maji can relate. Other
than the tiny raft he built by hand, Maji doesn't know a
thing about boats. He doesn't know how to steer or drop
anchor—hell, he doesn't know if all boats have anchors.
How are they supposed to travel in the dark? Or should
they sit there watching the unending darkness push
against the glass windows of the boat?

Maji's chest grows tight. There's so much he knows his father wants to say and that Maji has to answer for. But there's nowhere for him to run now. *So whatever is going to happen is going to happen now*, he thinks.

Instead, his father turns the key and the boat rumbles to life. Checking each of the meters on the dashboard, he grumbles, "We got enough water for a while. Might have some food, but I'd need to check. A first aid kit and flashlights are right by the door. Now if I only knew how much gas this thing has."

Maji feels the back of his neck flush with heat. "That's all you have to say? We're not going to talk?"

"We don't have time to talk."

"So you're just going to leave it? Dad, I ran away from home!"

He turns away from Maji and sets the boat in motion. "I said that this ain't the place. And I know what you did. But, hell, I'm out here trying to save you."

As the boat picks up speed, Maji steadies himself by leaning against the wall. He had thrown himself into the sea, into this journey, leaving everyone that claimed to love him behind. His father had rushed out to find him and now he didn't want to talk about it?

Maji thinks back to his home. How many times had he asked his father questions? How often had his mom gone quiet when Maji brought up his dad?

Maybe it's how close he's come to death. It may be how this trek out into the sea has aged him considerably.

Typically, when his father had brushed him away, Maji would back down and wait. In Maji's sixteen years, Eli has never raised a hand to strike him. It was always more about how his father commanded the room. This was a presence that took up all of the space—a threat.

It wasn't always like this. Maji and his dad used to be close. Eli would post Maji on his shoulders and walk around Manhattan, pointing out the tall skyscrapers and funny-looking clouds. It was like he never wanted Maji to walk—always wanted him close. Back then, Maji could read him the way he can read his mom. Maji can't remember the details, but he does recall how his father always gave off these beautiful blues and reds when he laughed.

This all stopped once Maji's legs and arms stretched out like taffy one summer. And suddenly, the warm tone in his father's voice disappeared with the piggyback rides. That rift grew and grew with each passing year, until the connection evaporated. Last year was the first of Maji's birthdays his father ever missed. After that, their relationship was never the same.

Maji feels empowered by making it this far. And so when he walks over, turns the engine off, and snatches the key, he stands there and stares, waiting for his dad to say something.

"I want to talk."

"Be quiet, Maji."

Maji feels an invisible nip on his neck like a struck animal. He can't help but ball up his fists.

"I'm not going to be quiet! I'm not a kid!"

"Maji . . ."

"I want to talk to you! Why don't you see that?"

Eli pounces on him. Maji throws up his hands as if to defend himself, but his father only puts his hands over Maji's mouth and presses him close to his chest.

"Just shut up for a second. Do you hear that?"

Maji can't hear anything but his beating heart. As it steadies, nothing but the chorus of waves beat against the side of the boat.

His father backs away, still listening.

That's when Maji hears two thumps against the side of the boat.

Three. Four.

Maji looks up at the windows expecting to see someone there, but all that greets him is the long night sky bathed by the moon. They both make their way to the back of the ship. Their boat is still adrift, but the waves have been strong enough to push it along.

Another thump starts at the front and climbs along to where Maji is standing. While his father checks the front of the boat, Maji looks into the water. There, illuminated by the moon's reflection, is a long piece of sogged wood. The large chunk clatters against the front end of the boat before spinning out into the open sea.

Looking at the water in front of him, Maji spots another broken piece that is longer and splintered along the edges. And another.

As his eyes get accustomed to the darkness, Maji spots hundreds of broken pieces of wood floating in the dark sea. There's also rope, blankets, and other objects drifting along the water.

Another large slab of wood passes by the nose of the boat. Maji sees his dad try to grab a piece out of the water, but it slips right by him. Then, remembering the flashlights in the cockpit, Maji runs to get one. Retrieving one, he shines a light at the giant mass in the water before the waves take it away. The sides have a metal post and a gray handrail running alongside.

"What the hell," Maji's father mutters.

When Maji casts his light beyond this mass of debris, he spots a larger piece sticking out of the water like a broken nail.

And this is when he realizes what these scattered pieces mean.

Maji and his dad are floating in a sea littered with what's left of their last hope.

The *Americana* is destroyed.

Chapter 23 ⇌

MAJI wakes up and because his body is so long, he almost falls off of the cot he's sleeping in. The morning brings a brilliant horizon that he has to blink through.

His father is at the front of the ship, staring out at the water. Maji takes his blanket and joins him. The air around the boat is warm, sliding its way across the sea's surface like a breath. The ocean is still as if it's listening for something in the sky. The pieces of the *Americana* are gone, swept away in the night.

His father hands him a rubbery brown package ripped open. Maji stares inside, and a slab of pink meat stares back.

"What's this?"

"It's a military meal, something they use in the army. I found a crate of them in the back. Trust me, that's the best one. Don't know what it's supposed to be, but it tastes like spam. How are you feeling?"

Maji takes a bite of the rubbery meat and hates it.

"The leg still hurts. And I think I have a fever."

After looking out into the water for a while, Maji asks the biggest question on his mind. "Do you think they survived?"

His father exhales. "I don't know what to think, Maji. I can't wrap my mind around what's going on out here. We just have to get home and figure it out from there."

Maji can't help but feel angry again. His dad had always pushed things off. He's left Maji out of most conversations, even when they affected him directly. He told him to stay away from the protests. He's kept him away from everything happening in the world. At first, Maji took this as his father wanting to protect him. *Leave it to the grown folks*, he would say. As a kid, this was comforting—a belief that someone with the power to protect you was on the job. But Maji started seeing the cracks in that statement as he grew up. *Leave it to the adults* started sounding like *You're too much of a kid to understand*. And that couldn't be farther from the truth.

His father places his palm on his forehead to feel Maji's fever. Maji finds the hand pressed against his skin as hard and cold as stone. "Let's get that first aid kit. Come back in."

His father busies himself by digging through the bright orange pack for supplies. Watching him, Maji can't help but feel like the gloom from the previous night is seeping into his pores. The entire crew of the *Americana*: Queen, Bishop, Norm. The thought that they could be dead weighs so heavily on him that Maji needs to lie down.

So much death.

So much.

The only thought he can hang onto, the only hope he holds in his heart, is that everyone was able to get off. Maybe another ship had come by. Perhaps they had gotten rescued.

Trying to swallow his fear is like ingesting a wad of thorns. It tears away at his throat. It shreds his lungs and stomach. When he pushes his eyes closed, tears spill from the edges and slide down his chin.

"Did you get anyone on the radio?"

Maji's father finds the pill canister and shakes two aspirins into Maji's hand. He doesn't even notice that Maji's face is wet. He's too busy.

"I haven't got anyone on the radio. But I figure if we can head East, we should hit something. Land. Anything. This ocean can't run on forever."

Maji wipes his face. "What about gas?"

His father gestures to all of the meters and dials and switches. "You tell me."

They both sit there in silence, but Maji knows what's going unsaid.

More than what had happened to the *Americana* and what had happened to its crew. More than how they were going to make it home without direction.

What is going unsaid is the mystery of what sank the boat and, more importantly, if they were going to avoid the same fate.

လ လ လ

Maji squints out onto the water, only to hear his father huffing behind him. "Still not wearing your glasses."

The comment is like a slap across Maji's face, but he doesn't want to show that it landed.

Instead, he says, "I don't see anything out there."

His father nods. "That's because it keeps disappearing. I can't explain it, but at noon, something showed up just on the horizon. So I moved us in that direction, and then it just . . . ."

Maji's father mumbles under his breath. He thinks that whatever's out there is a boat, maybe one so far that it creeps under the horizon. Maji keeps his thoughts to himself. Earlier on the water, he had seen the same thing just before the storm. *So it's still out there*, he thinks.

"There! Right there!"

He turns on the engine, and the boat flies forward, almost knocking Maji over. He stammers to get his footing before looking out of the window.

Sure enough, there is something out in the distance, but Maji thinks that it looks nothing like a boat. Instead, its silhouette reveals sloping edges too wide to be a ship. Even as they race towards the object, it seems infinitely in the distance as if mocking them.

Finally, after ten minutes, Maji's father switches the engine off and stares into the water. The object is gone.

"I don't get it. Do you see it, Maji?"

Maji isn't seeing where his father is pointing because he's too busy looking behind them.

"Dad?"

A few miles in the distance, the Atlantic seems to be bubbling. The fact that he can see this from this distance means that the frothing ocean must be kicking up into the air.

Maji hears his father gasp. "What is that?"

"It's right there."

"What is?"

"What I came to find. The miracle."

His father takes one look at Maji and then back out to the foam. But as they both look on, the water and air above it begins to swirl.

Maji's father grabs him by the collar and runs back into the cabin. "Get inside. We gotta go."

Right in front of his eyes, the swirling water becomes a funnel that reaches higher than Maji can see. The base of the storm swells wider and wider. The spiraling storm reaches up and impales the sky, turning the world into an ominous wall of dark clouds. Even though the sun is in front of them, a fierce storm is brewing some miles away. To Maji, it looks like pictures he has seen of an atomic bomb. The funnel-shaped clouds swirl as they touch the water.

As the boat takes off, Maji catches strings of lightning leaping around inside the base of the storm that is at least ten times larger than the one that sank his raft. The swirling face of this storm is so large that it moves like an impenetrable wall.

The ocean grows sharper and uneasy as their boat tries to outrun the massive storm. Maji watches as his dad tries to keep the ship in the direction of the shadow they saw before, but navigation suddenly gets difficult. The storm is still far off, but rain begins to fall—soft at first, and then, after a minute, sheets of rain like God was trying to flood the world again.

Without a line of sight, his dad yells, "Where is it, Maji?"

Maji can't find the words. The black clouds, which had been miles away at the beginning, were now right on top of them. The swirling funnel of the hurricane has caught up to them in an instant. The words are stuck in his throat.

"Maji! Where is it?"

"Everywhere," Maji replies, and suddenly all of the windows in the boat shatter.

The explosion knocks Maji to the ground.

As the winds whip around the cabin, Maji feels himself leaving the ground. He is weightless, and the boat is tipping. Suddenly, he feels his father pin him down with his body, and he hears him yelling, though the pressure of the air drowns out the words.

As their bodies rise towards the ceiling, Maji senses the boat being plucked out of the ocean and thrown into the air. The spinning almost causes him to throw up. But then they are falling . . .

Falling . . . .

Falling . . . .

And that's when Maji hears what his father has been yelling this entire time.

"I got you, Maji! I got you!"

Chapter 24 ⌐

WHEN Maji opens his eyes, his entire body screams in agony. He tries to sit up only to realize that his father's body is still on top of him. Finally, with a bit of leverage, Maji manages to slide himself free. Exhausted, he looks up and sees that the entire roof of the NYPD boat has been torn off as if by a mighty hand. The sky is blue, and there are puffy, white clouds in the sky: the exact opposite of the massive storm that had hit them.

Maji looks down at his chest and sees that he's soaked, not in seawater, but in blood.

Maji follows the trail with his eyes and stops at the back of his father's head which has been split open. Fearing the worst, Maji turns the man over only to hear his dad groan.

As he flops onto his back, Maji traces the bloody gash as it runs from the back of his head to his eye where the eyelid has also been torn open.

Shaking, Maji reaches out to him. "Dad?"

"That sucked," he replies and laughs. He touches the wound on his forehead and rubs his fingers together. "How bad do I look?"

Maji mouths something.

He sits up and leans against the broken door of the cabin. Maji is so shocked by the blood that he sees his father's lips move with no sound. When he realizes that his dad's been asking for a first aid kit the entire time, he scrambles to get one.

Though everything is thrown around, most of the cabin is still in one piece. From what he can tell, the boat hasn't taken in water. The first aid had been housed in a small metal box by the door. That box was now underneath the seat. Maji tries to pry the lid with his fingers, but the metal is bent. He takes a nearby slab of wood and jams it in between the cover. It pops open.

Under careful instruction, Maji spends the next thirty minutes bandaging his father's head. First, he binds the gauze diagonally around the wound in the back. He then cleans out the cut by pouring rubbing alcohol on the gash. Though the bottle clearly states not to use it on open cuts, his father insists. Finally, after some hearty F-bombs and whimpering, Maji carefully wads a compress on the injured eye and finishes wrapping his father's head.

"Well. How do I look?" his dad asks.

Maji nods. "Awful."

"Well then! With my eye and your bad leg, we'd make one hell of a pirate. Help me up on that cot."

The struggle to get his father's body off the ground tells Maji everything he needs to know about his father's condition: either the loss of blood or the blow to the head has made most of his body unresponsive. After laying him down, Maji looks for the aspirin bottle. When he can't find it anywhere, he tells himself not to panic.

It's not like dad's going to die.

"Engine still working?" his father asks weakly. He's lying on the cot sideways, his only good eye poking out from behind the flaps of Maji's poor wrapping.

Maji finds the key still in the ignition and gives it a turn. The engine half-turns, sputters, and then goes silent. Exhausted, his adrenaline finally coming down after the initial shock, Maji slips his hands over the side of the boat to wash them of dried blood. When he comes back, he sits right by his father's cot. His only eye is closed.

"Dad?"

"Yeah."

"What do you think happened to the *Americana?*"

His father stays quiet for a long time before replying, "We'll get through this. Someone will come. Get some rest for a bit. I'm going to . . . ."

His voice trails off.

And Maji is left staring at his father's chest as it slowly rises and falls.

∾ ∾ ∾

After an hour, Maji gets up to sift through the debris of the cabin.

He chucks the broken metal railings overboard. To him, keeping their sharp edges around is just asking for more problems. He finds a soggy box of those military meals his dad had offered him, but only two are left. He tears one open that reads "Chicken noodle soup," only to have it ooze out of the brown rubbery case. Maji dabs his finger in. *It tastes salty and looks like vomit, but at least it's good enough to eat.*

Maji finds something even more curious towards the back of the cabin. The leather is worn and exposed, and the book feels bloated, like an infected organ. As he walks back to his father and slides onto the floor, he flicks through its pages. The saltwater has ravaged all of the print, warping the ink so that the text is completely unreadable. Every single page is mashed between the leather binding. As his hand skims softly against the membrane-like pages, he finds it eerie holding this book—the only things he brought out to sea were this and his cell phone.

Maji's eyes light up. Crawling over to his dad's sleeping body, he shoves his hand into his breast pockets, jeans, and shirt. Maji pauses to marvel at the man's hand. So powerful, yet now lifeless. Intricate grooves outline the knuckles—scars his father would usually tout as his "reward for climbing out of the hood."

His hand brushes up against his father's gun holster; it's empty, but he still jumps back like he's touched an open stove. He finds the device tucked into a clip on his father's waist belt and flicks the phone open. There is a thick crack running diagonally across the screen, but it thankfully lights up.

With only five percent of the battery left, Maji goes to work. After flicking the airplane mode off and on and refreshing the map many times, a tiny red dot showing their last known location appears in the blue water. As he scrolls up, the map shows a sliver of land to the west. It's impossible to judge how far it is—an hour, a day—but it's there. Maji closes the map, and a nervous laugh slips from his mouth.

They aren't out in the middle of the ocean. They were close to land. He stands up to look out over the water but sees nothing. *The map says it's there. It must be there.*

When he looks down at the phone again, his dad's wallpaper is up. It's a picture of him. It's an old one, maybe by five years, but Maji remembers that day fondly. He is smiling as he tosses a basketball in the air. This was taken the day he had asked his dad to teach him how to ball. Maji always had this thing about playing ball as his dad did back in the day. But, unfortunately, a pretty wild growth spurt one summer had left Maji a somewhat uncoordinated mess when it came to any court skills. And even though the consensus was that Maji should stick to playing ball over Xbox Live, to him, this was a great day.

The ball is a blur in the picture, but Maji's sweaty, cheesing face is as clear as the sky behind him.

"That's my favorite picture of you," his father tells him. He is still lying on his side, but he's now awake.

"You got all grown after that. No more hugs and kisses for dad. No more big ol' smiles."

Maji shrugs. "I still smile."

"Mhm." After a long pause, he asks, "Found anything?"

"We're close to land. I think it's Long Island? Not sure. I can't see it, but your map remembers our GPS location." He looks at the man's prone body and sets his palm on his forehead. Maji's hand burns as if he's doused in boiling water. Shaking, he turns back to the horizon to see if there is anything he's missing. He turns the phone back on and waits for the map to load.

"What are you doing? That phone's not going to work."

"I need to get you back home."

His father laughs. "Who's supposed to be saving who?"

Maji doesn't find it funny. The map comes up, but there's no reception, no red dot.

"You're hard headed, boy."

"Yeah well. Mom says I get that from you."

Maji means this as both a joke and a backhanded comment.

"Mhm," his father repeats.

With only three percent left on the battery, Maji turns the phone off again. Part of him wants to cry, *But what is that going to do,* he tells himself. Maji's father sits up from the cot. He's groggy, but Maji knows he wants to say something.

"The day after you left, Maji . . . ."

"Dad—"

But the man holds up his hand. "Let me finish. Come sit next to me for a bit."

Maji reluctantly sits and pulls his knees close to his chest.

"The night you left, I tried to track you down, Maji. I went everywhere looking for you—asking for you. Wasn't easy. It's not like the city can keep track of every black kid that goes missing day by day. So I went on foot, checking every local bodega, hoping someone there had seen you.

"You already know how I feel about our neighborhood. Hell, I grew up in those projects. So I know what they can do." Maji watches as he wets his lips and folds his hands into each other. "I feel like it didn't affect me when you were just a kid. But as you grew up to be the young man you are now, I was reminded, walking those streets, that I hate it. I hate the way the roads lock around your neck like chains. I hate how the projects seem haunted by the kids who never made it out. But mostly, I hate how it makes me feel when I'm there: like I'm a product of my place in the world and an enemy to everyone.

"I wanted to be a cop growing up. I don't think I ever told you that. It was a way for me to protect my family. Get them out. But I could never get over the imposter syndrome." He laughs to himself. "Hell, I wouldn't feel like an imposter. I'd feel like a whole invasive species.

"The real cops weren't working as fast as needed, so I checked the spots you usually stop in. It took me over a day to find someone who had seen you. Amen, the bodega guy close to your school, told me he sold you a ton of snacks. He thought you were having a party or something. But then he said he spotted you with blue drums from the recycling site. It took me a day to get them to give me their security camera footage and another day to scrub it for you. I had no idea what you were building.

"Your uncle, Cal, works in the precinct in Brooklyn. Remember him? We used to go out to his house for Thanksgiving when you were just a kid. He told me that a call came through that a shoreline patrol boat had found a kid floating out in the Atlantic. He pulled a few strings to get me on the NYPD boat to get you. And here I am— ready to rescue you."

Maji listens to his father go through all of this with a lump in his throat. Then, when the man's hand lands on his shoulder, Maji looks at the veined skin, the strong digits, and the blood caked underneath the fingernails. Unlike before, the hand doesn't feel like stone on his skin. Instead, he feels its warmth and pressure. This calls to Maji like an echo of a distant memory.

"Why do you tell me all of this?"

The man lays back down.

"Because you wanted to talk. And because I wanted to tell you. Just in case..."

Just in case

And Maji knows the rest.

Chapter 25 ⌒

I'M sorry.

After spending seven hours on the still ocean, night comes. Maji stays busy cleaning the cabin and looking for resources as he grapples with the thought spinning in his mind.

Ever since his father told him how he found him and ventured out over the water, hoping to save his son, Maji has felt guilt festering under his skin. He repeats the phrase that's been on the edge of his tongue over and over again. Finally, he mouths the words. And while it tastes bitter on his teeth and gums, while it ties his stomach into a knot, Maji can't help but feel like time is growing short—for him, for his dad.

While his father rests, Maji fails to find anything to help them out of their trouble. No water. Barely any food. The cell phone is now down to 1%.

So when Maji speaks to his father, when he says the phrase that has taken over his mind, it seems to crackle the air around him.

"I'm sorry."

He sits and waits in the quiet of the ruined cabin as the ocean calls outside. Maji knows, just from his experience of being out in the water, that dawn is coming. A slight tear of light is awakening just on the horizon. Part of him wonders if his dad has heard what he's said until he asks,

"Sorry for what?"

"Nothing."

Part of him wants to drop the subject immediately, but his father sits up slightly and gestures to him. As Maji gets close, he sees that the bandages around the back of his father's head have been dyed a dull brown.

"Remember the first time you ran away, Maji? Wasn't that long ago. Last December. You got out of bed and left in the middle of the night, remember?"

Maji nods his head. "I didn't run away. Just went to Grandma's house. I-I needed a break."

He puts his hand on Maji's shoulder. Once again, this hand feels comforting, though he notes the weakness of the grasp.

"It's okay. I get it. My point is that you went missing. I had almost the entire precinct looking for you. Nobody could find you. But you know what I did? I stood in front of the building. We were in that deep freeze in New York. Windchill made it feel like one or two degrees that night. And you know what? I stood out there for hours waiting for you to get home. In my mind, you were going to come back because you didn't have any place to stay. So I spent the time practicing what I was going to say when you got back. How I was going to reprimand you. How I was going to ground you."

Maji watches the man blink his eyes as if he's trying to stay awake. Before Maji can ask, his father waves him off.

"Around hour three of waiting in front of that building, something happened. When I was waiting outside, a car pulled up and some people got out. They were from the building next door. They got out and pulled a girl, maybe your age, out of the backseat. She was kicking and screaming. They kept talking to her and trying to calm her down but she wasn't having any of it. Two people took her ankles and one guy took her shoulders and they straight-up carried her. Turns out she had run away and they had found her. The people who took her home were her mother and brothers and they just wanted her safe. They just wanted her home and she wasn't having any part of it. I remember seeing her and thinking, 'What's in the water tonight?' But the truth is, and it dawned on me in that second, that I didn't really know why you ran away. That even though you did something that I thought was stupid and put your life in danger, you must have had a reason for it. A reason you believed in. And I couldn't go and punish and get all riled up until I heard that reason first. You understand what I'm telling you here?"

Suddenly, a loud sound makes both of them jump.

The hiss of a powerful jet of water leaping into the air just a few feet from the boat echoes in the cabin.

Maji gets up to check on this noise, but his father grabs him.

"Let's go see together. I need some air."

Heaving his father's arm around his skinny shoulders, Maji lifts the man to his feet. But, unlike the first time, the more prominent man's body slumps down on Maji's, making it difficult to move. From what he can tell, his father's legs can't support his weight.

It takes all of his energy, but Maji manages to get them both to the edge of the boat overlooking the ocean. As Maji looks out to the black water with his father, the waves splash around them.

At first, there is no sign of the sound out on the ocean.

And then the first creature breaks through the surface.

At first, there are only three: Maji spots them some ten feet away, drifting silently on the surface of the water. Their backs are black and rigid, like the land below the surface has come up from the depth.

His father shakes his head. "What are they?"

A water jet blows outward from one of the blowholes. The others, as if communicating, call back.

"They're whales," Maji replies softly.

It's odd to see these creatures just floating alongside the boat. They seem both alien and familiar: as if born from a dream. Maji and his father stand silently, watching these creatures as they swim alongside the boat. And as if the world's weight lifts off his shoulders, Maji feels lighter.

"It's hard to explain why I came out here."

His father, still facing the whales, nods slowly. "You want to try?"

"Everything is . . . wrong. Nothing makes sense. It's too hard. Everything. It's like everything is shouting and yelling all the time. If it's not home, it's school. If it's not school, it's everything else. Just when things make sense, it all falls apart. You and mom, my classes, my friends. Every day, I get angry. That's all. I get angrier and angrier."

"You sure it's anger?" Eli asks.

"Did you hear what I said?"

"I heard you, Maji. I'm just saying. Sometimes we confuse anger with fear."

"I'm not afraid of nothing!" Maji yells. His body is shaking. The strain is too much. His pulse is racing. The ocean's roar seems to be coming from inside of him—an impossible wave of pain pours out of his skin.

Limping over, the man leans down and presses his bandaged forehead against Maji's until the trembling stops.

"I get afraid."

"You do?"

Maji hears him chuckle. "I'm always afraid, Maji. Being afraid is what we use to stay alive in this world. It's what we are taught back home. Watch your back. Trust no one. But when I grew up, I realized that fear eats away at you. It feels … it feels like you're on fire. Like you're breathing in fumes. You ever felt that way?"

Maji nods his head as his father's breathing becomes heavy.

"And you just want to tear everything down. With your own bare hands, just rip it and ball it up. Because of your fear, you want to be in control. And the only way you can be in control is by burning the whole thing down."

These words claw at Maji's chest. They feel like the answer to a question Maji has never asked. And the man who had that answer is slowly dying in front of him.

"I thought you hated me," Maji admits nervously.

He watches his father's only good eye begin to tear. As the tears streak down his cheek, he says, "Maji. I can never hate you. The person I hate is myself because I don't know how to protect you. I *can't* protect you."

Anger and fear. Maji wonders about the line drawn between them. When are they different? When are they the same? Like his father, what Maji had confused for anger was actually the fear of losing everything in his life. Maji realizes that though he was suffering alone, he wasn't the only one.

After a long silence, he musters up the most difficult question—one that comes tumbling out of his mouth with every ounce of pain and doubt left in his body.

"When we get back to the city, are you and mom going to break up?"

Maji's father doesn't reply right away. Instead, most of his weight is right on Maji's head.

"I don't want to leave. You understand that?" And then he adds, "The real reason I told you that story from before, the one about me waiting for you outside in freezing weather, is because I stood out there for five hours, Maji. Five. And then I picked up and drove to your grandma's and found you there, didn't I? *I* found you, Maji. I did. Not your mom. Not the other officers. Me. I did. Just like I found you out here. That has to show you that I can understand. That I want to understand you, Maji."

Maji's eyes fill with tears. "I can't go back, Dad. I can't . . . ."

"What happened, Maji? Did something happen?"

Maji slips back into the cabin to retrieve the book. When he finds it, he holds the book close to his chest like he can't breathe. "I thought I could find it out here, but it doesn't exist. Just like this old book. It used to have writing in it. It used to have a story, but there's nothing in it. There's nothing. It's all gone."

Maji tosses the book overboard, and it splashes into the ocean. Sinks. Vanishes.

"There's nothing. Nothing special out here. Nothing for me back in the Bronx. Not in school. Not on the street or my friends. You and mom are . . . ."

Maji grips the side of a boat but the rest of his body curls like a match blackened by fire.

Just as he's about to let the grief swell over him, Maji hears his father exhale before collapsing.

With his face stained with cold tears, Maji tries to wake him. When he doesn't get a response, Maji tries to drag his body back to the cot but finds it impossible. So Maji settles for padding the floor with blankets and rolling up a shirt for a pillow.

Both emotionally and physically exhausted, Maji staggers outside and throws his arms over the ship's side.

The whales are still there, rising and falling beneath the water's surface. Maji watches them for so long that the light catches him by surprise when the sunrise sparks a new day on the horizon. And as the new day illuminates the water around them, turning the cold, green waves into sharp angles of gold and silver, Maji realizes that there are more whales out there than he had first thought.

Hundreds of whales—some the size of small cars, some double the size of the boat—swim around the broken vessel.

And not just whales: dolphins leap and flip into the air; starfish wade effortlessly on the surface of the water like children clasping hands; blue constellations of jellyfish skim along the skin of the sea; giant turtles, with their spotted fins and brown-stained shells, bump up against the boat. Above the small ship, the sky is mobbed by hundreds of seagulls, swirling and screeching over the pounding waves.

And there were other creatures, too—creatures Maji had never seen before. Long-necked fish with wavy, white beards that make them look like dragons; octopi with long tentacles and barbed suckers; creatures that look like seals but with impossibly long horns jutting out of their foreheads.

When the whales collide with the boat's frame and start pushing it along the water, the force nearly knocks Maji to the ground. The ship's wood groans as if it's about to split open under strain, but the hull stays intact.

A feeling of hope fills Maji's chest. He had put himself and his entire family in danger, but now he wants to risk everything to save them as they are. To see New York City again. To see his mom again. And he is going to—one way or another.

"We're going to be okay, Dad," he whispers, but he quickly regrets speaking these words aloud. Instead, he looks out in the distance and sees the crest of white vapor rising into the air some twenty feet as if the ocean is on fire. This wall of water grows so high that it blocks the new day's light.

And Maji knows, *It's here.*

Chapter 26 ❧

T HE entire ocean begins to tremble and the entire host of sea creatures dip back below the surface and vanish. The sky, which was once littered with screaming birds, opens up as they scatter to the wind. The entire ocean has dragged Maji's broken boat to the foaming sea. And now that they have been brought to this place, the creatures of the earth have vanished. Now the hot vapor rising into the air is gone.

There is stillness.

A quiet.

At first, Maji finds the change in the sea minor. The height of the waves is less powerful than before. The crests are no longer white at their peaks. The hills scattered across the ocean are just now starting to level. Even the warbled sound that comes from the sea begins to die into a whisper. The wind stops blowing. The world creaks still and silent.

Maji watches as the water becomes a flat, unmoving surface as if it has been transformed into a sheet of glass. Even the broken ship's dark metal pieces and splintered wood sit impossibly still on its face.

Maji can't believe what he's seeing and backs away from the edge. But, when he looks up, it seems that even the clouds in the sky have frozen in place.

The world is mute.

Suddenly, just ten yards from the ship, something rises from the water. At first, it's only a hard patch, like the water has grown a lump of hard, gray skin. But it then spreads outward, parting from the still water almost forty feet across.

Terrified, Maji trips over himself as it rises and continues to rise, high into the air like the sea has given birth to a mountain—a new world. The remaining stars, the ones still fighting against the waking day, dress the sky as the clouds part.

From Maji's perspective, the prominent wall of scarred, white hide is large enough to blot out the sun. The front section is predominantly snow-white with hundreds of hideous marks around the front slope that, for some reason, remind Maji of the deep tissue scars on his father's worn knuckles.

At this moment, Maji recognizes this creature for what it is. It's a whale—a whale so large that it defies everything he's ever known. Unimaginable. Mighty. Impossible. He loses the word for it on his tongue and in his mind. He looks into the distance, seeing the ocean cascading off its hide in grand waterfalls. The beast is so long that just its size seems to make the horizon buckle.

The whale begins to turn, as slow but as deliberate as something as massive as this can be, causing the waves from its wake to nearly drown the tiny boat. Maji watches the broad, white mound of its head pass, only to stop at what he immediately figures to be the beast's right eye.

The darkest part, its pupil, seems deep and endless that a plane can seemingly fly through the blackness of that tunnel with ease. Surrounding it are gray clouds of pigment which appear torn from an actual storm.

Maji feels tiny and crippled staring into this darkness. Maybe it's because the eye is so massive that he sees the entirety of the boat in its reflection. Or perhaps it's because within this eye he feels there lies power and understanding, lost language, rage, and misery. He feels this. It pours out onto him like the burning core of a volcano. In its gaze, Maji feels like he's withering and incomplete.

Up close, the scars on its skin look more like murals of

suffering. Maji doesn't know why but these shapes remind him of the world he knows. One deep scrape looks like the screaming mother holding a child. One shape is oddly curled like the C2.0 sign-off he knows so well. Maji can't tell if this is all in his mind.

Finally, the whale finishes its slow turn and glides away. The sky above Maji's sight line bends like the creature's weight is pulling the air on a tide.

Trembling, Maji stands and starts to back away. While he wants to run back and check on his dad, his eyes dare not break away from the creature casting off like an ocean liner. But just as he feels strong enough to turn away, the whale, not many yards out, heaves down into the ocean. And with that movement, the tail section of this creature rises to the sky. It's at least ten times the size of the boat across, from fin to fin.

Maji expects it to drop down and follow the whale's body underwater, but instead, it keeps rising until it's jutting out of the water, completely vertical. The fins are so high up that clouds disperse away from their edges. The shadow casts a calm wind over the boat and the ocean for as far as he can see.

Realizing what's about to happen, Maji hurries back and drags his father's lifeless body into the cabin. His arms and legs feel like they will snap, but he uses the blankets to move him. He pushes his back against the wall under one of the desks and bounds his legs and arms around the man's prone body.

The clap against the ocean tells Maji that the tail has luckily not fallen on the boat. But the impact sends glass and shrapnel around the cabin. The explosion is so massive that it changes the weather itself.

Maji finds himself weightless as the ship tips forward in midair. They are so high that he can see, just beyond the cracked windows, the clouds, now drenched in salt water, let out a moan that immediately incites a storm.

Black and gray clouds swirl as the boat is pushed forward by what feels like a massive wave. A tsunami! Smaller parts of the ship tear from their posts due to the force, but most remain whole.

The howling of air . . .

The roar of the ocean . . .

And then suddenly, Maji's stomach drops as the boat plummets. Then, with his legs still gripping his dad, he interlocks his arms around the metal posts and prays that it holds.

The boat makes a violent splash-landing back into the Atlantic. The vessel's front is instantly crushed like a tin can on impact, and water flushes right into the cabin. Maji tumbles to the other end of the small room and cracks his head on the edge of the table. Dazed, he hangs on for dear life. With his father's body still in his clutches, he hangs on to what he knows he loves the most.

A second wave picks up the ship. A wall of water approaches: taller than a house, frothing at the edges. It draws so close that Maji can no longer see its peak.

He remembers the sound of the water landing on the boat like a giant sledgehammer.

He remembers feeling the walls and floors implode.

He remembers holding his father one last time.

Chapter 27 ⌒

WHEN Maji wakes, he immediately turns to his side and wretches warm water from his nose and mouth. The wet heave is painful to the point where Maji feels like his very soul is being torn out of him.

As the final heaves subside, Maji digs into the ground to feel the sand funnel up between his fingers. He scoops up some of the brown clumps and stares as they fall. Finally, his eyes focus enough to see that he's surrounded by sand—he's on a beach.

Waves crash nearby, and Maji instinctively scurries back as the hissing edges climb up the shore. Barely managing to get to his feet, he feels every inch of his body cry out in pain. Dry blood stains his shirt—an intense bite of an object is buried into the meat surrounding the tip of his elbow. Instead of caring for this, Maji turns his mind to the world around him.

There's still daylight, though the sun will soon set again. He is on a beach, standing among the scattered pieces of the broken boat. The dune runs back for many yards until it meets a steep rock wall that reaches out from overhead. Beyond this, Maji can't see what world lies just beyond it.

And then a panic sets in.

The memories flood back into his mind.

The wave. The storm. The explosion. The whale.

The whale . . .

Panic spreads along his chest, and he feels like he's drowning again.

"Dad? Dad?"

Nothing but the crashing waves reply.

"Dad? Dad?"

Pain makes it hard to see, but Maji fights through.

The boat was cracked open like a cheap toy, and its guts were scattered along the beachhead. Tons of its trash is still washing up on shore, but this doesn't stop Maji. Even with his left arm bleeding, he pulls open every metal slab and checks under every fractured wooden piece. Even as his cold, beaten body tries to betray him—Maji works his joints and muscles, knowing that if he stops even for a minute, the exhaustion will take him.

When Maji's adrenaline is gone, he stumbles but refuses to fall. Then, up ahead, he spots the most intact piece of the ship lying on its side.

He enters the cabin, but he's only greeted by darkness. He fumbles around on his hands and knees, checking every corner, every pocket, but his father isn't there. When he crawls out of the twisted doorway, he sees, in the distance, that sunlight is slowly coming to an end. And framed by this, he sees an object pulled in by the tide. It seems small and fragile but curled on a wooden frame. The waves kick at it and embed it into the sand, but then they claw to drag it back to sea again.

Maji runs as his voice lets out a wail.

Lying unconscious on a small square of floating wood is his father. The ocean manages to pry the wood from the sand and drag the boards back out to the waves, but Maji is there to grab him before the sea reclaims him. Fighting through the pain in his arm and legs, he scoops up his father's body and pulls him back to the beach where they collapse in a heap.

Maji checks his vitals. His heartbeat is faint but present. Unfortunately, he's not breathing.

Maji remembers what he was taught in his school's first aid class. His high school mandates that all students take a CPR course, but Maji barely paid attention during those classes.

He goes into chest compressions. He loses count after the fifth but still gives his father the breath from his lungs.

He doesn't even think twice. But, unfortunately, the man's chest barely rises.

Maji doesn't stop. His compressions are stronger now, deeper. He throws his back and arms into it. When Maji gives him a breath from his lungs, he gives him everything.

The chest rises.

Suddenly his father begins to cough up water.

As relief settles in, Maji turns him over to his side and rubs his back . He feels, under his hand, the heavy body of his father as it wrestles with the pain of coming back, but now he's laughing. His father was there when little Imajin took his first breath, and now he's there for his.

At this moment, a thought comes to him, and it's like he can hear his mother's voice for the first time.

Maji can hear the music, her laughter, too.

Do you know why we named you, Imajin? Do you? We always knew that we were going to love you, but we didn't always have a name. The day you were born, we were all sitting in the delivery room. And you had just come out, so the whole room was looking at you. The nurse and the doctor took one look at you, and I can tell that they thought you were the most beautiful thing they had ever seen. I could tell by the way they smiled and laughed. They glowed. And when I held you, you opened your eyes. You weren't crying, and once you looked around at everyone, it was like you could see their happiness, too. Like you could feel their joy. And that's when you, not even a minute or two old, smiled back. As big and as bright as day.

That's where your name comes from. Because you mean so much to me and your dad. We knew, from that moment, you were going to have a big heart. A heart that could feel every-thing. That's what the world needs, you know—more people who can love and cry and laugh. That's our dream for you, Imajin.

Your love will be magic.

Maji cradles his father as the man looks up at him.

"You got us home?" he asks weakly, but with a dull laugh behind it.

"I got you, dad. I got you."

It's the only thing Maji can repeat because his tears are dripping down onto the man's face. Maji can also see the blue colors surrounding his father's smile again. He feels at home. He feels loved. Maji knows that he's holding something truly magical. By some miracle, by something along the lines of God or gods, they had made it back to the world.

Maji hears voices all around him. Then, finally, someone shouts from the top of the cliff. From over the edge, Maji sees hundreds of faces peer down—black, white, brown.

They are all calling to him.

His father stirs. He seems fragile in Maji's arms, but his smile puts one on his face. He struggles to his feet, and Maji helps him walk to the voices.

As they get to the brush line, Maji feels the heat rising on the back of his neck and turns. The sun has broken into the water and is now an orange ball of pure beauty. And there, clasping the edge of the world, is the whale. Even from this distance, the massive body dominates the horizon. The sun frames its white skin like a burning halo. The spout of water that shoots into the air turns a pocket of the sky into storm clouds.

Maji turns and sees that he's not the only one who sees this.

His father's face is a mixture of awe and horror.

Maji turns his back to the ocean and carries his father into the rushing crowd of people. The faces on the cliff are also looking out to the water. They are pointing and shouting. A helicopter buzzes overhead and holds its position over the masses.

Now they can all see and know the majesty of the ocean.

And yet Maji keeps walking, holding his father. He feels the steady pulse of warmth between them, basking in the warm glow of the most beautiful day he has ever seen.

Without realizing it, his cheeks are wet.

Maji had gone out to sea and found his miracle.

About the Author

Alcy Leyva is a Bronx-born, multi-genre writer whose first two books in the Shades of Hell series, *And Then There Were Crows* and *And Then There Were Dragons*, were published by Black Spot Books. His short stories have appeared in the award-winning anthologies *A Midnight Clear* and *Dead of*  *Winter*. He currently lives and teaches in New York City.